KU-489-599

Dakota Guns

Jack Thorn was a hunter and had been since the remnants of Quantrill's Raiders, under Captain Charlie Chiles, had killed his wife and child. There had been thirteen of them. Now, only Chiles was left and Thorn was still on his trail heading towards the Dakotas.

Here the Sioux were squaring up to Custer, and Thorn's old commander, General Hipman, was defending the beleaguered Fort Burr against all comers. No longer content with murder and raping, it seemed Chiles had a new line selling guns to the Sioux.

If only Jack could track Chiles down, he would prevent the greatest disaster the West might ever know.

Dakota Guns

MIKE STALL

A Black Horse Western

ROBERT HALE · LONDON

ISBN 0 7090 7802 1

Robert Hale Limited
Clerkenwell House
Clerkenwell Green
London EC1R 0HT

Typeset by
Derek Doyle & Associates, Shaw Heath.
Printed and bound in Great Britain by
Antony Rowe Limited, Wiltshire

PROLOGUE

Summer 1876

Jack Thorn sat alone in the bar drinking his coffee and listening. Even the barkeep had long since deserted him for the spectacle outside.

Well, nothing much happened in places like Crossville, Indiana, and a double hanging was an occasion, so much so that they'd put it off until noon for the convenience of the spectators and the extra trade. But very soon now this bar would be just as crowded as it had been an hour ago.

Even, Thorn guessed, hosting the hell-fire minister, thirsting prodigiously after his alfresco service culminating in the hanging itself – the two convicts led to the gallows in a hushed silence, shuffling up to it, snarling or sobbing at the minister as he proffered to them the Good

Book to kiss in repentance before the black hoods were fitted and then the nooses over them as they stood on the brink of eternity. The bar would not be graced, however, by any members of the Women's Committee for Decency, their usual anti-drink placards replaced by ones bearing a single word: Shame! That had intrigued him on the way in and he'd asked about it. Oddly, it wasn't the execution they objected to but the fact that it was being held in public for all to watch. Thorn found that puzzling. If you were going to hang a man surely it was better to do it in public and not in some hole in corner way? No matter: it was a free country. And his purpose had been achieved last night when the county sheriff had let him talk to the two condemned men. Just to one of them as it turned out. The other had already given up talking for eternity, mute in his hatred. But Josiah Kelly had been in terror of his meeting his Maker and itching not only to confess, unnecessary now, but to tell what he knew about his one-time leader, Charlie Chiles. It . . .

Silence. All the distant noise had died, only expectancy remained. Thump! That was the mechanism of the gallows itself, not the falling bodies, but indicative enough. The silence persisted. Chances were one of them was kicking now, his neck not broken by the fall but fighting for air inside his black hood.

Thorn felt neither sympathy nor pleasure at the notion. Instead he reached into his pocket and brought out the papers which he set out on the table before him – a folded dodger, a newspaper cutting and a list of thirteen names, ten of which were already crossed out.

He reached for his pencil-stub to cross out two more, stayed his hand. These two weren't dying now for what they had done in New Mexico Territory but for a bank robbery here – a most inept attempt at that. They hadn't even got the money outside the bank but they'd still shot and killed the bank guard. If this weren't Indiana and civilized, they'd never have seen a trial and a scaffold; the nearest tree and a pair of lariats would have done for them.

His eye fell on the cutting.

SANTA FE SUN-TIMES
EX-QUANTRILL RAIDERS
SACK HACIENDA
Seven Murdered including Mrs J Thorn
And Son Thomas
A band of *guerrilleros* under the command of self-styled Captain Charlie Chiles struck terror into the heart of New Mexico, laying

waste the hacienda of Captain Jack Thorn, a noted local war hero and veteran of the great victory at Wiggins Landing, serving under Brigadier-General Hipman. Captain Thorn was still *en route* from Washington when the dastardly raiders struck . . .

He looked away from the cutting abruptly. He surely didn't need the reminder. Suddenly his hand scrunched up both list and cutting and, after a moment's hesitation, he threw them on to the already well-littered floor of the barroom. The pencil joined them a moment later. The thirteenth name wasn't one he was about to forget and its expunging would take more than a pencil strike. But the dodger – the wanted poster – he put back in his pocket. He suspected that it might still prove as useful as the gun on his hip and the money belt about his waist.

Outside the sound came fully back – not loud, there was no more singing now, just normality returned. The men were dead. He stood up and walked swiftly out of the bar to where his horse was hitched up to the rail. He unhitched it, mounted and rode off, not looking back once to the place outside the county sheriff's office where the scaffold had been set up. That business was done with. Now only one name remained – Charlie Chiles. And he wasn't to be found anywhere in Indiana. For that he had to go north, to the Dakotas.

ONE

There was something about Lucky Nugget he didn't take to. Like most mining towns it had an air of impermanence but to Jack Thorn it already felt like a ghost town with people in it.

That was unimportant in itself but if you couldn't trust a place it was hard to trust its people either, so he didn't risk going straight to the marshal's office. He might end up giving information out and receiving none back, and that he couldn't afford to do. So instead he went to the biggest saloon.

It was called the Lucky Strike and it was pretty basic. The floor was of rough wooden planks which creaked when walked upon; the bar was unpolished pine and the only furnishings were locally and roughly made tables and chairs. There wasn't even a mirror behind the bar. A dump.

'Coffee,' he told the barkeep.

'Sure thing,' the barkeep said, 'we've some on.'

'Hell, mister, you too young for whiskey?' asked one of the patrons. He was about twenty and pretty drunk. Thorn just looked at him. He went quiet. So did most when Thorn showed that kind of interest in them.

The barkeep, who had stepped in back for the coffee, returned with a mug of java. It was black and very strong. Thorn complimented him on it.

'Heck,' the 'keep said, 'it's all I drink. If'n I drank what I sell I'd be dead these five years.'

Thorn smiled slightly. 'I'm looking for a friend.'

'Ain't we all?' the barkeep said.

He'd got a joker. Thorn smiled even more slightly.

'Goes by the name of Charlie. Average height, reddish hair, a scar on his left cheek.'

What's his last name?'

'Usually, Smith. There's a wide choice.'

'Naw, I never seen him round these parts. What about you, Willy?' This last to the drunk who had gone silent.

'Reckon not,' Willy said.

Thorn finished his coffee. He reached into his pocket.

11

'First's always on the house,' the barkeep said.

'I'm obliged.'

'Fancy way of talking,' the barkeep said. 'You some kind of Reb?'

So, despite the humour, the barman was keeping up old animosities. Thorn went instantly on the attack.

'Who did you serve with?'

'Hell, I was on the frontier—'

'I put on a blue coat and defended the Union,' Thorn said crushingly. He reached into his pocket, tossed a coin on the counter. 'Good coffee.'

Outside, Thorn cooled himself down. He was getting short of temper these days. That fool of a barkeep wasn't worth troubling over. And worst of all, he'd learnt very little but had given out information concerning a man with a scar. Chiles would know he was still being searched for if he heard that and he well might.

But how could you look for a man without asking questions? He ought to know by now but he didn't. He'd got this far because most of them had been fools. Chiles wasn't that.

He walked across the street to the bank. It had a printed wooden sign:

THE CONSOLIDATED MINER'S BANK
Wilse Kefauver, President

and was of the same light frame construction as the rest of the town, which intrigued him. How could you keep money safely in what amounted to a wooden shed? Inside, Kefauver – who also served as teller, and presumably swept out too – was only too pleased to show him. A safe.

It had been fixed to the bedrock by iron bars which also embraced it, leaving only the door free.

'It's the very latest from Baltimore,' Kefauver said. 'You could maybe blow it apart with dynamite but you'd gain nothing at all, sir, nothing at all! The gold dust would be all over town and a dozen very angry miners and store-owners would be closing in on you with shotguns.'

'I wasn't considering it,' Thorn said.

'Oh, I'm sorry, just a way of speaking, sir. Besides, that letter of credit you've just shown me enables you to gain access to its contents at any time and perfectly legally. But also not everybody believes in proper withdrawals and we have to remember that!'

'You do indeed,' Thorn said, holding back a smile. The small, fiery man wasn't exactly your usual banker. 'But I shan't be using my letter of credit today. I just needed to make sure you could honour it.'

'No trouble at all, sir. This is a coming place, Mr Thorn, believe me. There's not only the miners, there are ranches. Horse ranches usually but turning more to cattle now the war's over. The war *ate* horses, sir, ate 'em up.'

'I know,' Thorn said, remembering.

'You fought for the Union too, sir?'

Thorn nodded.

Suddenly Kefauver's hand was out again. 'Sergeant Kefauver, New York volunteers.'

Thorn took it. 'I was in the cavalry.' Nothing too precise about that but he decided not to lie if Kefauver pressed him as he might well do. This damned town seemed obsessed still by the war. Most other places, the ex-Confederacy excepted, preferred to forget it. But he was saved by the advent of another customer, a miner with a bag of dust.

Kefauver retreated behind the counter, weighed the dust on his scale.

'Six ounces exactly, Harry. Do you want cash?'

Harry Whoever-he-was glanced at Thorn, questioningly.

'It's OK, Harry, Mr Thorn here is a valued customer.'

'I just need fifty bucks,' Harry said, nodding to

Thorn who nodded back.

Kefauver refilled the bag, tagged it, wrote Harry a receipt and went to the safe. A key appeared in his hand as if by magic. Thorn watched as the deposit was made and cash extracted. There was nothing casual about the transaction. Kefauver could have been a priest of the altar. He was surely right about how safe the bank was – one yell from him and the town would be about the ears of any would-be bank robber.

Harry disappeared, dollars in hand, presumably to celebrate in a saloon. But cautiously – fifty bucks' worth and no more. Thorn didn't doubt some gambler would get most of it eventually but he'd have to take his time and go carefully. Harry was wearing a gun but he looked more the type of man who preferred using his fists; he had shoulders like a bull.

'I'd better be going,' Thorn said. 'One thing, Mr Kefauver. I'm looking for an acquaintance. His name's Charlie. A middle-aged man, reddish hair, about my age, scar on his cheek.'

Kefauver scratched his head. 'Charlie . . . ?'

'Smith, usually,' Thorn said, essaying a smile.

Kefauver smiled back as if not quite knowing why. Then: 'Reddish hair, scar on his left cheek?'

'That's the one,' Thorn said with forced casualness.

'Yes, I saw him. About a month back.'

'A miner?'

'No, not in here. It was in the Belle Union and only the once. Probably just passing through.'

Thorn didn't press him. Kefauver had obviously told all he knew. It was time to go back to the saloons.

Which yielded nothing. Thorn didn't hold back this time. It would be all over town somebody was looking hard for a scarfaced man but aside from Kefauver it seemed no one had seen him. He then sought out the town marshal, a little reluctantly. Thorn didn't rate town marshals highly. They were usually just promoted bouncers and always in somebody's pay.

Marshal Carey was perhaps the exception that proved the rule. He was oldish, with an engaging manner but he was not a man to be taken lightly. He didn't carry a six-gun but a double-barrelled sawn-off in a holster. He didn't need to be fast with it – just fire it and somebody got cut in half.

'You got a dodger?' he asked. There was nothing for it but to show it. Carey merely glanced at it, then nodded to the pile of wanted posters on the desk in the small office.

'It's in there, pretty old too. As I recall there were thirteen altogether for the one crime

16

before most of them were recalled. A bit unusual.'

'Yeah.'

'A thousand dollars each, except for Charlie Chiles.' He handed the dodger back. 'Three thousand dollars. Hell, a man takes notice of that kind of money.'

'You've seen him?'

'I saw a man with a scar,' Carey admitted. 'I didn't put it together though.' He paused. 'I'm sorry I didn't but it still mightn't be your man. Lots of men with scars about these days.'

'And red hair?'

'And cold blue eyes. He was riding with a straw-haired man, middle height, broken nose, didn't look none too bright but I wouldn't vouch for that. They weren't miners or ranchers so I kept an eye on them in case they'd thoughts about the bank. Heck, there's damn all else worth robbing in this town. They stayed an hour or two, rode on.'

Thorn realized Carey had just told him who really paid his salary.

'Do you know where?'

'West. They could have been going straight ahead for the Indian agency or intending to fork north for Fort Burr or maybe they were on their way to Canada.'

'I'm much obliged, Marshal.'

'For what?' Carey paused. 'There were thirteen dodgers. Then one by one they were called in.' He looked at Thorn. 'You paid out much?'

Thorn shook his head.

'I reckoned as much. It was your family they killed?'

'I was coming back from a posting in Washington. I'd survived the war and had just resigned my commission. I was going to raise horses and cattle and kids for the rest of my days . . .' He broke off. 'I heard Chiles was in the Dakotas from Kelly and McGillis, just before the state of Indiana hanged them.'

'But they didn't all hang, did they?' Carey said.

'No.'

'Be careful if it's Canada. That dodger doesn't mean much up there.'

'Legally it doesn't mean much here, either,' Thorn said. 'But with Chiles it doesn't matter. The army still wants him for running with Quantrill. And he won't go to Canada yet.'

'How do you know?'

'I've hunted him on and off for almost a decade, Marshal.'

Carey nodded. He knew about hunters.

'Incidentally, who's in charge at the fort?'

'Hipman.'

'General Hipman?'

'No, just a plain major.'

Thorn said nothing. It couldn't be the same man.

'Do you think this Charlie Chiles will try for the bank?' Carey asked suddenly.

'If I thought he would, I'd stay,' Thorn said. 'But he won't. It looks a lot easier than it is. The whole town would be after him. He'd have to be mad to try and he's not mad, just bad.'

Carey nodded 'I reckon you're right.'

Maybe, Thorn thought. And maybe not. . . .

The Indian Agency was a tiny village – the house, the agency itself, stables, storehouses, corrals – but it was also a deserted one. There was no one about, no cattle in the corrals nor horses, some of the buildings had a slight air of neglect to them, and most of all there was a distinct lack of Indians – not even a solitary tepee between here and the skyline.

He tied up at the hitching rail in front of the house. The garden had a few blooms in it but they too had a half-hearted air to them. Poor soil, good enough for the grass but little else.

'*Señor?*' The door was opened by a rather

squat Mexican woman, almost as far from home as he was.

'I'd like to see Mr Roman,' he said, using the name Carey had given him.

'Come in, please. Miss Jane will see you. Come through, *señor*, she's in the parlour.'

Thorn gave her his hat, walked over a polished wood floor into a large, lightly furnished room. A woman of about twenty-two or -three was sitting by the window, the light on her long auburn hair. She sat with a straight back, her hands in the lap of her everyday brown dress, her face virtually in shadow. Thorn suddenly realized they'd seen him coming from over a mile off across the plateau. This was a plain woman's pose, showing herself to her best advantage. And then she stood up and walked over to him, offered her hand.

Thorn was a little slow in taking it for he now saw her face and she wasn't plain in the least. She had startlingly light-brown eyes, a retroussé nose and a flawless white skin.

'Ma'am,' he said.

She looked a question.

'My name's Thorn, Jack Thorn. I'd like to see the agent.'

'I'm sorry but he's out. Maybe I can help?' She smiled. 'Oh, I'm sorry, Mr Thorn, I'm Jane

Roman. And please sit down.'

Thorn took the indicated chair and was relieved she didn't take the one she'd favoured before. She sat opposite, ten feet off.

'I wanted to ask Mr Roman —' he began.

'It's Dr Roman.'

'My apologies.' He paused, then: 'It's a good idea having a doctor as the agent. It should be done more often.'

'Oh, he's not a medical doctor.'

Thorn looked a question.

'He was a professor at a New England university. He's a PhD, not an MD.'

Thorn was silent a moment. His easy assumption had turned out to be a gaffe, revealing that Dr Roman had come down in the world, and if his daughter wasn't about to admit it, who could blame her? The trick now was to change the subject as quickly as possible.

He said: 'I didn't see any Indians as I arrived.'

'They're out on the plateau, five miles further west. There's better water there for their numbers and my father permits it.' She paused. 'He's there now but he'll be back by evening. You would be most welcome to join us for dinner, Mr Thorn.'

Thorn hadn't intended to stay but he could hardly refuse now. It might seem as if he were

21

demeaning the doctor further.

'It would be a pleasure, ma'am.'

And then the Mexican servant arrived bearing a tray of tea and cookies. He hadn't drunk tea for years and a similar gap was in order for the future but he still complimented her on it and refrained from dunking the cookies in the thin liquid.

She was, without doubt, a truly handsome young woman. That was worth the difference between a cup of tea and a mug of coffee, or even a shot-glass full of rye. His own Elise had favoured tea, he recalled. And scarcely conscious of doing so, he found himself comparing the two. . . .

Dr Hector Roman wasn't at all what Thorn had imagined. Unconsciously he'd been expecting a slight – and slightly effete – creature with at least a hint of failure about him. Roman was built like a small blacksmith, and as they stood on the veranda smoking his – not very good – cigars, Thorn also found that his conversation had nothing intellectual about it.

'You were in the army, Jack?

'Yes, sir.'

'For God's sake, call me "Roman" – not Hector, that's a name for a dog!' He laughed. 'I was too old for the war myself and I wasn't sorry. I was born in Delaware, brought up in Virginia, trained in New York and I taught in New England. I would have felt wrong whichever side I fought for.'

'I was on the Union side, Roman,' Thorn said softly.

'So was I, if that matters. Teachers of philosophy don't win battles.' He paused, then: 'But you're probably wondering what I'm doing out here. Rum sort of cove for an Indian agent, eh?'

'Indian agents usually are rum sort of coves, sir.'

'Roman! – but you're right. And there was I, fancying I was different!'

Thorn laughed. It was hard not to like Roman.

'But I was telling you why I'm here. Indian languages, boy, Indian languages! Hundreds of 'em and most not recorded. It was my hobby. So when I was passed over for dean of college, I thought – why keep stuffing young heads with philosophy they don't understand or even want to? So I wrote to a few of my old pupils who'd done well for themselves in government and here I am.'

Bluster? Thorn drew on his cigar. Maybe, and the longer you listened to him, the more Virginian his accent sounded.

'What are you doing tomorrow?' Roman asked suddenly.

'I'd been thinking of heading for the fort.'

'Good. It'll still be there the day after. Come with me to the Azat camp – "Azat's" their own name for themselves, by the way – they're always interested in that at the fort.'

'I'm not a serving officer, Roman.'

'Aren't you? You have the manner of one.'

Thorn smiled. 'Blame West Point and then a civil war, but I resigned my commission in 'sixty-seven.'

Roman looked him over. 'So what do you do now?'

'I ranch out in New Mexico territory.'

'In between searching for someone.'

Thorn said nothing.

'Do you think I haven't seen hunters before? Or that I didn't learn to understand the men I taught in college? For instance, you ranch in a large way. Your clothes are travel-stained but new enough and top quality, ditto your horse. For that you have to ranch in a big way. No small ranch could sustain a hunter who's away half the time. And it's personal as you obviously could afford to buy it done.'

'You're a clever man, Roman.'

'I like to think so, but it doesn't do me all that

much good. I sometimes think the stupid have it better. Nothing worries them.'

Thorn shrugged. 'You wouldn't swop.'

'Of course not.'

'And maybe you've seen the man I'm hunting.'

'Maybe, but it'll have to wait.'

'Why?'

Roman nodded towards the door where Jane was now standing.

'Dinner's ready,' she said.

Thorn just looked at her. She was wearing a green dress cut from some sort of brocade, quite simple, but with the lamplight behind her and the orange of the setting sun on her face, she almost took his breath away.

She turned suddenly and disappeared into the house. Roman clapped him on the back.

'Come on, it isn't done to keep a lady waiting.'

Thorn followed him in, wordlessly.

Thorn sat on the guest-room bed and looked out of the window into the night, featureless save for the stars. Dinner had been almost a disaster, and yet very nearly a success too. They hadn't talked business until they were well into coffee and cigars – the house was dry, not a drop of liquor in it.

'No, sir, I haven't signed the pledge,' Roman had said smiling, 'but I'm a philosopher by training and avocation so I'd be a fool to confuse my own thinking apparatus with spirituous poisons. Jane isn't a philosopher but thanks to me she's never got the taste for it.' Jane had smiled at that and Thorn too. 'Now tell me what or, more likely who, you're looking for.'

So he had, not holding anything back. These weren't people to gossip. And he'd almost got a result: a man fitting Chiles's description had passed through a month back posing as a photographer. He'd even expended some plates on the Indians before leaving, to the west.

'Into some trouble,' Romana had added. 'The Sioux are at daggers drawn with the army there, and General Custer and General Terry are on campaign. Maybe a stray bullet will do your work for you.'

And he would never know. Perhaps the expression on his face had betrayed him for suddenly Jane had called him a damned fool – not in those exact words though; she'd done it in a very ladylike way but still with a touch of anger underneath.

He'd heard much of it before, revenge was a fool's quest, and an arrogant one too; it was a form of playing God. But her anger hadn't stemmed from that source What really had seemed to annoy her was the fact that he was throwing his life away, and that had seemed to upset her mightily.

He had scarcely argued. Maybe she was right. He could have put it all behind him, married again, lived on the fat of his land . . . if he had been someone else. He'd spent four years killing people he didn't hate in his country's cause. Spending twice as long killing those he did in his own cause had never seemed excessive, and it hadn't been continuous anyway. Once he'd gone a whole year on the hacienda, worried about water supplies and Chicago beef futures, the trail effectively cold, and then the news had come that two ex-Quantrill men had been taken and were about to be hanged in Indiana. It had been like coming back from the dead.

Roman had understood. When Jane had taken her leave – a little earlier than usual, Thorn guessed – he'd offered his help:

'Come with me to the Azat camp tomorrow morning. Zanai will know where this Chiles is if he's still in the region.'

'Zanai?'

'The Azat chief. He's the one this putative Chiles supposedly took a photograph of.'

'In all his feathered regalia?'

27

'I wasn't in on the session, but it's no sillier than a top hat.' He'd paused. 'You'll like Zanai. You're not unlike.'

Thorn hadn't enquired just how. According to some, the Indians were Nature's gentlemen; to others, wicked savages. Perhaps it was best to let it lie there cloaked in decent ambiguity.

Best of all now would be to sleep. Tomorrow he set out on the Chiles's trail again, a coldish one but still a trail. He lay back on the bed. After a moment he turned off the lamp.

There was little to see as they rode, just naked grassland punctuated only by a few well-separated hillocks with a hint of mountains on the horizon. Thorn would have ridden in silence, out of habit, but Roman was a talkative man.

'You'll have noticed one thing about the agency,' he said.

'Probably,' Thorn replied.

'I mean, no cattle.'

Which was true. No people, no cattle. To live here the Indians needed supplies, dry-goods and cattle, and there had been none of the last.

'I get cattle sent up monthly. I don't keep them at the agency and dole out slaughtered meat. I let the Azat have them and do their own slaughtering. The Bureau of Indian Affairs wouldn't approve.'

'Count on me not to tell them,' Thorn said.

'Now I'm obliged,' Roman said, adding after a moment: 'I've gotten rather fond of the Azat.'

'That's the Sioux clan living hereabouts?'

'According to the Bureau. According to themselves they're not Sioux at all, just allies like the Cheyenne. They speak a very different language.'

Thorn knew Indians spoke a whole host of languages and, to combat mutual unintelligibility had even evolved a sign language of some complexity. But what particular doomed language the Azat spoke really didn't interest him. It did Roman:

'I think, my fried, that the Azat language is Indo-European.'

'Like Latin and Greek?' Thorn asked, somewhat incredulous.

'And Sanskrit, Persian and English too. I believe the ancestors of these Indians came from the ancient Ukraine. I'll show you my notes sometime. When they're eventually published they'll cause an almighty academic storm.'

'Do they look different from other Indians?' Thorn asked practically.

'No, not at all. Perhaps I put it wrongly. It's not about race, just about language and if I'm right it will provide a new insight into language itself.'

It struck Thorn that you could take the professor out of academe but not the academic out of the professor. Still, it did no harm. Plenty of Indian agents exploited their jobs, gave out insufficient stores, watered their beef and pocketed the profit. Roman's enthusiasm at least ensured he treated his charges decently. He said:

'Tell me about Zanai.'

Roman smiled, as if realizing he hadn't made a convert.

'He's about my age, a great fighter in his day but grown cautious with age. That's why he's not with Crazy Horse and Sitting Bull. He knows the reservations are the only hope for his people.'

'And he'll talk to me about Chiles?'

'Why not? If, that is, he knows anything. Which I doubt.'

'You'll translate for me, Roman?'

'No need. He speaks English.'

That last proved to be an exaggeration, or Zanai was being intentionally obtuse. He was a tall man for an Indian, almost six feet, nearly as tall as Thorn himself, and he still held himself like a warrior though age had creased his face into a maze of lines, but his dark eyes still gleamed with intelligence.

'Chiles, yes, man with box that draws. Came, went. No hear more.'

And that was it. A fruitless journey. Thorn left Roman and Zanai to their business and walked around the large village. No one bothered him: the fact that he'd come with Roman seemed passport enough.

It was much like every other Indian village Thorn had seen, though cleaner than some, and the women and children looked better fed than in most. That surely was down to the tiny herd of cattle grazing to the west of the village, courtesy of Roman. And from hunting too. He saw several guns. The Bureau issued guns to Indians for hunting, mostly fowling pieces though one of those he saw was a Springfield caplock, the rifle they'd fought the war with. So what? You needed a big gun to bring down an elk and war surplus guns were cheap.

He stood a moment and watched an old man cleaning the barrel of the caplock. He was doing a very professional job; the gun itself was in fine condition, not gleaming like the ones you did drill with at West Point but then you never, ever fired such guns. They were drill guns, for show. This was for use. And then he noticed the marks on the wooden butt, almost burnt off but not quite obliterated.

Thorn turned and walked back to where he'd left Zanai and Roman about their business and took his leave. Roman looked disappointed that he wasn't going back to the house with him. Zanai didn't hide his indifference.

Thorn found his horse, mounted up and rode off, resisting the temptation to look back and, above all, the urge to ride off at a gallop. There was probably no danger. The marks had been nearly illegible and there was no reason for any Indian to realize he'd noticed them or worked out what they meant. There was no reason to believe any Indian had noticed them at all; they were just squiggles to them, just three faint Anglo letters: CSA – Confederate States of America.

Thorn was certain the Bureau of Indian Affairs wasn't supplying the Indians with imitation Springfields used a decade back by the Rebs. But somebody was and Roman wasn't the man to tell, either. But he knew just who was.

TWO

Fort Burr stood at the head of the floodplain of a lost river, separating the Azat Plateau from the Broken Hills of the miners, and proudly defending the United States from Canada to the north. Such was the theory but it had been a lie to begin with and was now plain foolishness. If anything the Sioux provided a better defence than Fort Burr ever could and even in the War of 1812 nobody had ever thought of fighting it out this far west.

The fort certainly wasn't impressive at first sight. A middle-sized stockade stuck in the middle of nothing just about summed it up. It was totally vulnerable to artillery, easy to surround with infantry, but for all that, Thorn was still very glad to see it.

The guard at the gate admitted him without enquiry. Thorn walked his horse over to the HQ office and hitched it to the rail. He stepped inside. The duty corporal at his desk glanced up at him, not even deigning to formulate a question. This was army territory and civilians came a long way second.

'I'd like to see Major Hipman.' The sign outside had, amazingly, confirmed the rank and the person.

'Business?'

'Urgent military business, Corporal,' Thorn said, putting a touch of West Point snap into his voice. 'Tell him Captain Jack Thorn is here.'

The corporal was on his feet instantly. 'If you'll wait here, sir.'

But it was not necessary. Hipman had already heard and was opening the main office door. He'd changed a little. There was a touch of grey in the hair and a few extra lines about the mouth but the massiveness, the certainty of the man, remained.

'Jack, are you back in the service? What the hell, come in, come in!'

'As you say, General.'

'It could mean nothing,' Hipman said, sipping the coffee Corporal Dawson had brought in for them. 'You only saw the one rifle after all. And the Azat Sioux would be mad to start something

34

now with the number of troops already in the Dakotas. The Sioux proper will be submitting soon enough. General Terry has got comparatively huge forces at Fort Abe Lincoln along with overall command of Custer's Seventh Cavalry, and further west there's Crook and Gibbon. Besides which, Zanai hasn't been in the field. He'd be a fool to start something and that he's not.' He paused. 'What did Roman say?'

'I didn't tell him.'

'You don't trust him?'

'Oh, I suppose he's loyal enough. He insisted I accompany him there. But I got the impression he'd take Zanai's word before mine.'

'Hell, you really do believe it!'

'Yes, sir.'

'Then so do I. You were the best staff-officer a general could have, Jack.'

'What happened to the rank, sir?'

Hipman laughed. 'I was just a wartime temporary brigadier-general. I never expected to keep the star but at the end they just didn't need officers of field rank who'd risen through the ranks. They would have made me a captain again if they hadn't been careless enough to have given me a brevet majority after the Tall Pines battle. A kind of compromise was struck and I got sent

35

out West.' He paused. 'You should have stayed in, Jack, afterwards.'

'You know why I couldn't.'

'Yeah, find Chiles and I'll hang him for you, if need be.'

And Hipman could and would. This was federal territory. Being taken in arms against the Union was cause enough for summary justice.

'One thing,' Hipman said. 'What's in it for Chiles – just his general enmity to the Union?'

'No, there has to be money in it too. Have the Azats access to some? From the Sioux, say?'

'They live on other people's beef,' Hipman said. 'And the fabled canyons full of gold are just that – fables. There are no Eldorados. There's some placer gold at the workings but no Indians pan for it.'

'So I could be wrong, seeing plots where there are none.'

Hipman put down his coffee cup. 'It would be the first time, Jack. Assume the rifle was a sample, that Chiles was hoping to use Zanai as an intermediary with the rest of the Sioux.'

'A few dozen Reb rifles wouldn't be of much account against Gatling guns,' Thorn agreed.

'They rarely are,' Hipman said, 'but a few hundred would be a whole different kettle of fish indeed.'

*

Jane Roman walked back from the storehouse carrying a bag of sugar. It was baking day and she was going to make cakes. Her father enjoyed a good Dundee cake and Juanita didn't have the knack, nor the taste for it either. To her it was more fruit than cake. Maybe she was right.

Except Jane found she didn't really care about the cake at all, Dundee or otherwise. All she could think about was Jack Thorn and how angry she was with him. Which didn't make any sense as he was nothing to her nor ever would be – and that dinner had been a disaster. She'd as good as called him a fool and then, like a fool herself, flounced out. In the morning when he'd left with her father they'd barely exchanged a word.

'Ah, *el azúcar*!' Juanita said as she entered the kitchen.

'It's sugar,' Jane snapped back. 'Call it sugar!'

Juanita smiled. 'So we talk English. And what do we talk about in English, little one? Cakes, the weather or just maybe *el señor* Thorn?'

Jane banged the bag down on the table, spilling some on to the clean surface. Juanita moved quickly, brought a bowl, retrieving it.

'I'm sorry, Juanita,' Jane said after a moment.

Juanita smiled. 'Is good you are angry, little one. I worry about you, alone out here with just me and your father.'

'I was vile to him,' Jane admitted.

Juanita shook her head. 'No, you were worried for him. I hear everything. So you think men can care for women who only simper at them?'

'I don't know. It just seemed such a waste of life.'

'Is honour. *El honor es muy importante.*'

And suddenly Jane was in tears. Juanita held her, comforted her.

'Tears are good, little one, let them come. He will be back, never fear.'

But even as she heard Juanita's comforting word, she wondered. You catch more flies with sugar than vinegar, and this man Chiles whom he sought, whom he had pursued for so long, would not be easy in the taking. He might kill him. But somehow she didn't believe that. She just couldn't imagine Jack Thorn losing. Ever.

It would have been easy to slip back into army life, Thorn thought as he walked the plain to the north of the fort. He'd just found himself noting slight dips and rises, important to an officer defending the fort, not to a mere transient. Hipman had asked him to stay longer while he found out what he could about the rifles, and you didn't refuse a man like Hipman without good reason, but if there was one certainty in the world it was that Charlie Chiles was never going to visit an army post of his own volition. In fact, Thorn could no longer see what Chiles would be doing here in the Dakotas. Giving guns away to the Indians out of the goodness of his heart and to stir up rebellion? Hardly, even the most irredentist of Southerners would be on the side of the bluecoats when it came to an Indian uprising.

Maybe he really was on his way to Canada. He'd stolen enough in his life to be rich but Thorn still doubted he was. None of the men with him had died rich; in fact, they'd all died dirt poor. Chiles probably wasn't that but you couldn't carry too much gold on a horse when the US Army and every sheriff north of the Mason-Dixon line were after you. So not Canada. He fervently hoped so. A man could really lose himself there.

There was always the gold in Lucky Nugget but only a fool would try to rob that bank with less than half a troop which he assuredly didn't have, so it had to involve the Indians.

He glanced down at the land, not as soldier now but as a rancher. It was poor soil, too poor for anything but grazing. The few ranches around might well raise fair horses and cattle but rustling wasn't Chiles's style. The livestock slowed you down and fetched little enough cash anywhere but at a railroad.

Thorn smiled grimly to himself. Not even for a moment could he put Chiles out of his head. He'd been toying with the idea of going back home, waiting for news there, but he now firmly rejected the idea. Chiles had probably moved on but if he were in the gun-running business it probably wouldn't be with the Azats but using them to get to the Sioux to the west. So west it was, via Lucky Nugget, though when he'd next cut trail on Chiles he had no idea. Dakota Territory was big, wild and mostly empty. But if Chiles were here, he had to be too.

Hipman watched Thorn from the battlements of the fort. Jack was like a hunting dog straining at the leash, he thought, and almost envied him. At least he wasn't just passing time. There was a battle coming out west but they'd left him here to hold this place. General Terry hadn't even bothered to turn up here, just sent a first lieutenant with an order that had stripped him of one of his two cavalry troops and his two six-pounder field pieces. That left him without artillery and just a scratch troop, together with the cooks and bottlewashers of the fort personnel – eighty-three men in total.

Worst of all, Terry was right to have left him here. The campaign was going to make careers so why waste the opportunity on someone whose career was effectively over?

The business of the CSA rifle was troubling but probably nothing. His Crow scouts certainly knew nothing of them and he'd had no reply on the subject from General Terry at Fort Abe Lincoln, but that was probably because the telegraph lines were down again. The Indians didn't like the 'singing wires' which was also very useful for binding the handles of knives and for quite a few other purposes. He wasn't even sure Chiles was hereabouts. Red-haired men with scars were common enough after a war fought by great numbers of men of Irish descent on both sides.

No, the chances were Thorn was wasting his time and his life chasing a phantom. Hipman took out a cigar and was about to light it when he heard a noise from below. He turned, saw a dispatch rider at the gate talking to Lieutenant Tidyman, his executive officer. But they were doing more than talk, they were shouting. What in hell was Tidyman doing engaging in a shouting-match with a common trooper? Hipman thought, as he put the cigar back in his pocket and started descending the somewhat rickety steps.

But they weren't shouting at each other he realized, as his foot touched terra firma, they were just shouting. Something about the Little Big Horn and Custer. Some damned nonsense or other, he thought as he walked with purposeful step towards the gate of Fort Burr.

THREE

Charlie Chiles touched the thin, white scar on his cheek. When asked, it was an old bayonet wound from the war. In fact, a tree branch had cut him during a wild escape from Union cavalry but he preferred the lie. Lies were usually preferable.

'It doesn't matter,' he said.

Dogget shook his head. 'They'll hang us!'

'Only if they catch us.'

'But with Custer dead—'

'The damned fool may even have done us a favour,' Chiles said, pausing to glance out of the line shack window. Nothing. He continued: 'Five hundred rifles. Tell me, if they were found on your land, how would you explain it? You couldn't. There's only one explanation: to sell to the Indians. But now the Indians think they're winning and are desperate to buy, we push through a quick sale and who gets all the blame?'

'The Indians,' Dogget admitted.

'The army will be very angry indeed with the Sioux,' Chiles said. 'They've killed two hundred and fifty of their men and a famous general to boot.'

'He was only a short colonel,' Dogget said.

'On the muster rolls, no doubt, but in the New York papers he'll be a general again, never doubt it. And a general commands an army so an army has been lost. The republic doesn't like losing armies, even mythical ones.' Chiles smiled suddenly. 'Come to think of it, this could be called a patriotic duty. By selling the Agat Sioux guns, we're destroying them utterly.'

Despite himself, Dogget smiled. 'Not a defence I'd care to mount in court.'

'With half of the twenty-five thousand dollars we'll get in your pockets, you'll never need to. Only the poor get judged, it's what they're there for.'

'And we'll have struck a blow for the South,' Dogget added.

Chiles nodded. He couldn't say it but he no longer gave a damn about the South. He'd

always preferred it to the Yankee North but not
so much so that he'd ever been prepared to die
for it, which was why he'd joined the irregular
cavalry. Raiding in Kansas was infinitely safer
than charging massed bayonets in the
Shenandoah Valley. After Quantrill had left on
his mad journey east to kill Abe Lincoln – not
only did he get killed in Kentucky, a mad actor
beat him to the punch! – Chiles had taken the
rest of the band west, intending to get to
California and a decent anonymity. He could
have achieved it too if it hadn't been for that
hacienda in New Mexico Territory.

Ironically, it had not been at all to his wish or
intent. Why stir up great trouble for little gain?
Haciendas didn't drip with cash, just cattle, but
they'd been a hot-headed bunch and at the time
he'd been their captain mostly by riding in front
and leading them where they wanted to go. And
how was he to know the owner would be absent
and take the loss of his family so personally and
obsessively? Those damned reward posters had
killed off any chance of blending in with the rest
of the immigrants in California. Or any place
else these last ten years. But this one coup
would give him all he needed to make a clean
break – wealth. That it would also cost hundreds
or even thousands of lives didn't interest him.

They'd all die eventually and so would he: what mattered was that he enjoyed the time in between.

'So nothing's changed,' Dogget said.

'Nothing. I'll make the final arrangements.'

'I'd still like to know who's your link to the Indians.'

'Maybe you'll find out soon enough.'

'You can trust me now,' Dogget said.

'I do, my friend, I do. He, alas, doesn't trust anybody but me; he can't afford to. And I've given my word.'

Dogget nodded, giving in.

He thinks I'm frightened that, being the middle man, I might be cut out, Chiles thought. Fool, but it was better that he was a fool, much better. They gave much less trouble at the end.

Outside, Auguste was waiting, leaning against a fence post smoking a hand-rolled cigarette, his straw-coloured hair almost hidden by his cut-down sombrero.

'No problems?' he asked.

'Not for us,' Chiles said. Then: 'Shall we go and visit the enemies of our enemies?'

Auguste grated the cigarette to fragments between thumb and forefinger and started for his horse. 'A pleasure.'

His pleasure was always in others' pain, Chiles

thought. A weakness, at least theoretically. But not in Auguste's case – at least, not yet. He was so good at it. He mounted up himself. They'd a fair ride ahead of them.

Lucky Nugget had proved anything but. This time, with the news about Custer out, he'd not been in the least reticent, even showing the dodger and buying many drinks, but he'd got nothing beyond a dubious confirmation that Chiles had passed through with a blond fellow who might be called Gus something or other. But his hunter's instinct said Chiles it was, so the place to go next was Fort Abe Lincoln. Hipman, in the light of the new situation, had wanted him to stay but there was nothing for him to do there and he'd met General Terry in Washington after the war and got on well with him. Guns and Indians would interest him even in the middle of a campaign.

He nooned early. There was no rush; it was a long ride to Fort Lincoln especially as he'd have to circle well south to avoid the Sioux reservations. He ate sparingly – bread, cheese and water. It would only be the first of quite a few cold camps but he was used to that from the war. The solitariness was something different but he'd plenty of experience of that too this last decade and he'd almost got to value it. To be out alone under the big sky, hunting his man— Hell, was he getting to enjoy it?

It seemed disloyal to admit it, even to himself, but the answer had to be yes. He was very, very good at it and it needed doing. That said, he would still be glad when it was all over.

He took out the makings, rolled a cigarette and lit it with a lucifer, watching the clouds boiling frozenly over the distant low hills. It was one hell of a world. Who would have thought of General Hipman set to commanding a no-account fort in the back of beyond? Or a girl like Jane marooned on the plateau. . . .

He shied away from thinking about Jane. Just as he avoided thinking about Elise still. That hurt too much, always would, and it wasn't disloyal not to want to get hurt. You had to be very sick indeed to enjoy pain.

The cigarette was burning his fingers. He scrunched it out, let the remains fall to earth. It was time to be moving on . . . but someone else had the same idea. There was a horse and rider coming out of the west and not too slowly either. He went over to his horse, checked his handgun and the Winchester in his saddle sheath, mounted up and then saw it was quite unnecessary – it was Jane. He rode out to meet her.

'I didn't expect to see you again,' she said, staying her horse but not dismounting.

'You looked to be in a hurry,' he said.

Her face tightened. 'It's my father. I'm going to town to find him.'

Thorn shook his head. 'I've just come from there. He's not there.'

'Are you sure?'

He nodded, then: 'Is he missing?' It sounded vaguely stupid. Of course he was. But all the same she said:

'We haven't seen him since yesterday morning. He said he might have to go to town after the Azat camp so when he missed dinner we thought . . .' She shook her head. 'He's never been missing like this.'

'It's probably nothing. He'll have stayed with the Indians.'

'I suppose so.' She didn't sound convinced.

'I'll take you back home and go look for him.'

'I'll go myself. You can come if you wish.'

'It'd be better if . . .'

She turned her horse. 'I'm going,' she said.

Thorn shrugged. He didn't like it but he couldn't order her around. And something about the set of her face said he'd better not try.

'I'll ride with you then, ma'am.'

She didn't reply, just set her horse in motion.

*

Jane rode well, something he wouldn't have expected. He kept pace with her but didn't try to lead. It was her father who was missing, not his. All the same, when they reached the rocky hillock that was the last bit of cover before the Indian village, he rode ahead.

'Let's stop here.'

She did but mutiny was visible at the edges of her mouth.

'Look,' he said, 'if there's a problem we don't have to make it worse. If there isn't, the horses get a couple of minutes to rest.'

'What problem?'

'We'll know if we see it,' Thorn said. 'Humour me, Jane. It can't hurt and you never know.' Without waiting, he dismounted.

Thorn would have climbed the rocks on his own but Jane insisted she come too so he helped her, though it was hardly necessary. They reached the top and then the village was spread out before them; it seemed almost near enough to touch.

'Oh, he's there!' Jane said in relief, pointing. There were three men standing outside Zanai's tepee – the owner himself, Roman and another man, a man with a prominent scar on his cheek.

There was a wooden case at their feet. Zanai bent and took an item from it – a rifle. Thorn would have bet his life that it bore the letters CSA on its butt.

'Let's get down—' Jane began.

'No, and be silent,' Thorn said, indicating that she kneel beside him. She didn't argue this time and as they watched it soon became apparent that the men were arguing. Roman was waving his arms about, doubtless his lecturing style.

'I don't understand,' Jane said.

'Wait,' Thorn said. She hadn't recognized Chiles and he didn't care to explain. If she weren't here he would have fetched his Winchester and finished him but he couldn't put her at risk. Besides which, it would be suicidal. Their horses were tired, the Indians' wouldn't be.

Roman took hold of the rifle, almost tore it from Zanai's grasp and cast it down. He was shouting but he was too far off to hear. All the same, it was easy enough to guess. He was arguing against using the rifles in the present situation. It was good advice too but it wasn't taken. Chiles picked up the rifle, handed it back to the Indian. Roman protested, Chiles knocked him down and as Roman knelt there in the dust, Zanai brought the butt down on his head, once, twice and Roman lay there, obviously dead.

Chiles laughed, full throatedly, his head thrown back, and Zanai joined in.

'Oh—'

Thorn reached out instantly, clamping his hand over Jane's mouth and pulling her back out of line of sight of the incident. After a moment he asked: 'You won't scream?'

She shook her head. He took his hand away.

'We've got to go to him. He could be—'

'He's dead. You saw it.'

She obviously wished to argue but she didn't. She'd seen the ferocity of the blows. Roman was dead and believing anything else was wishful thinking. She still gave in to it. 'But—'

He put a finger to his lips. 'We aren't out of it ourselves,' he said. His first inclination was to get the hell out, head for the fort on the spur but there could be more still to see and Hipman needed to know just what. 'Keep dead quiet,' he said and tried to see what was happening below.

They just left the body to lie there in the dust of the village while Zanai was handing out guns to his braves. Each one received a small bag, probably of caps alone or maybe of caps and cartridges. Then orders were given and six of them moved off and were soon mounted up and riding – directly towards them!

Jane had moved back to where she could see, sensibly keeping low, and he heard her sharp intake of breath.

'Lie down,' he said softly, doing so himself.

'The horses—'

'They won't see them from the trail,' he said in a whisper. 'Don't let them see you. You know what they'd do to you, don't you?'

She obviously did. She made herself small. Thorn did likewise. Captured, he'd probably end up envying Roman.

And then they were past, gone. He ventured another glance at the village but Chiles and Zanai were gone too, either into the tepee or elsewhere, he didn't know. The now empty case of rifles lay beside the undisturbed body of Roman.

'Jack,' she said very softly.

'Yes?'

'What are we going to do?'

It was a good question. They needed to get to the fort. Hipman had to know what was afoot. But there were Agat Sioux to either side of them now. Jane was a pretty fair horsewoman but that mightn't be enough.

'We wait for dark,' he said.

'And then?'

'We start for the fort.' He paused. 'I think

we'll make it.' He looked back once more. There was nothing now to see. 'Come on, let's get back to the horses. We can wait there.' They'd be better hidden too. He helped her down, noticing her self-possession though her cheeks were wet with tears.

Back with the horses he unshipped his Winchester and sat beside her with the gun over his knees. There was no gun-sheath on her horse and he considered giving her his six-gun, decided against. The chances were she'd not hit anything and he could make better use of it himself Anyway, if they were found they were dead anyway.

It seemed to take forever for night to fall. She took some water but refused food. He didn't press the matter but he ate some cheese and bread. He knew out of long experience that the wise soldier ate whenever he could. He also reflected that perhaps the really wise soldier got himself turned into a civilian at the very first opportunity. But somehow the joke didn't seem all that funny.

'It's dark enough,' he said at last. 'Mount up.'

She did so and in the fading light he saw the resolution in her face. The tears were gone but her eyes were cruelly sad. She shouldn't have had to see that.

'Follow me,' he said, 'and if I tell you, ride like the devil for the fort.'

'What about the agency?'

'No.'

He saw a 'but' form on her lips but ignored it. She saw the reason for not going home an hour later. The blaze had died down a little but it was still bright enough and an enormous pall of smoke hung over it, blanketing out the stars.

'Juanita!'

'There's nothing to be done for her,' Thorn said, not looking at her. 'Come on, let's ride!'

'Mr Tidyman, I'd be obliged if you would escort Miss Roman to her quarters – Lieutenant Gosport's will serve in his absence – and see Mrs Raney on the way. Ask her to provide for any feminine necessities at my charges.'

'Yes, sir.'

Jane looked appealingly at Thorn.

'You'll be fine,' he said. 'I have to make my report to Major Hipman.'

She nodded, complied; the door closed behind her.

'Now,' Hipman said, 'suppose you tell me what really happened.'

'Everything happened just as I said. Jane Roman saw most of it too, as you heard.'

'Hell, it doesn't make sense.'

'It'll make sense for the newspapers and if I'm ever called on to testify I'll repeat it word for word. But here, between us two . . . ?'

'Go ahead.'

'I think Roman was Chiles's connection to Zanai. He spoke the language and I reckon he'd always been a Southern sympathizer. He said he'd left his college for want of promotion. I'll bet he was fired. But he'd been fairly careful and there was nothing in his record to stop him getting a job with the Indian Bureau. Heck, his sympathies probably got him it, somebody helping out a fellow Virginian.'

'You mean a plot in Washington?'

Thorn shook his head. 'No plot at all, just pull. I dare say he was a pretty fair Indian agent in the end.'

'A bit on the soft side,' Hipman acknowledged, 'but he worked hard.'

'For a pittance. He was a clever man, sir, and here he was with his daughter, stuck in the wilderness with no prospects for either of them. Chiles is sly; he exploited his Southern leanings and tempted him with the prospect of good hard cash. He fell.'

'So why kill him?'

'Zanai performed the actual deed but it's my

bet Chiles instigated it. Why share? As for Zanai, I reckon it's a declaration that he's joined with Crazy Horse and Sitting Bull. Roman was the nearest available white man.'

'His own private Custer,' Hipman said; then, 'Autie dead! Hell, it doesn't seem possible.'

Thorn shrugged. It seemed all too possible to him – Custer, he of the long hair and the hard ass had always been too fond of cavalry charges. This had just been one too many.

'Why not kill Chiles too?'

'The rifles. There was just the one case there. I reckon the first rifle I saw was a solitary sample and the case an advance to enable them to get the money to buy the rest.'

'By taking this fort? Small money they'll find here!'

'By attacking Lucky Nugget and taking the bank. Chiles couldn't do it himself with just one man but a band of Indians mostly armed with caplock rifles could, and I estimate twenty-four rifles in that case.'

Hipman nodded. As Thorn had guessed, he'd worked that out for himself. You don't rise from private to general, however briefly, without being able to see things as they are.

'But that's not all the rifles, is it?' Hipman asked. 'How many all told?'

'Probably around five hundred. Zanai hasn't that many braves but he'll get them from other tribes if he has rifles to give out.'

'And I have some eighty men, most of them just serving out their time, and a fort and a town to defend.'

'Zanai won't get the full consignment until Chiles gets the gold. It won't be a simple exchange, either; Chiles values his scalp.'

'So stop him getting the gold and it all fizzles out?'

'There'll be some fighting whatever. Zanai has killed a federal official and he'll have some guns. Heck, the government gave them some for hunting.'

'Maybe you're wrong, the guns were at the agency and he already has them.'

'Chiles is no fool, sir. The guns are hidden somewhere, probably on one of the ranches. He's been planning this for a while, and rather well. He gets the gold, he gives Zanai their location, the rancher gets the same as Roman and Chiles goes north to Canada a rich man.'

'And all this happening under my nose,' Hipman said

'Not at all, sir. The official version is that Chiles is just a renegade and a gun-runner who's exploiting Custer's defeat. Roman's innocence works for you. You might even get to be a general again.'

Hipman laughed aloud, then: 'I wonder whether you'd be pushing your cock-and-bull tale of the brave Professor Roman trying to talk Zanai out of fighting if his daughter was fat and forty.'

'I hope so,' Thorn said. 'Chiles has ruined too many lives already. She's lost everything, but as a traitor's daughter . . .'

Hipman was silent a moment, then: 'It happened just as you said. Now, how do we beat Zanai?'

'By holding out, both here and in Lucky Nugget.'

'Easier said than done. What about the town? The miners will fight – they're mostly ex-soldiers – and they're armed after a fashion already.'

'They'd fight better with a troop of cavalry to back them up, and one man definitely in command.'

'Right, Captain Thorn, you're back on the payroll. I'll give you half a scratch troop and a few spare rifles if you want them. You defend the town.'

Thorn shook his head. 'I'll go with them but I can't command. I'm not even in the territorial militia. I'm a civilian.'

Hipman smiled. 'Damn the manual of military law. I'm the officer in command and I can do anything I have to, to win. And I need you in command there. Terry took all my officers except Tidyman and the doctor. Tidyman spent the war in Vermont procuring horseshoes. I need a fighting soldier.'

'But—'

'And the fort is closed as of now. You leave it in command or not at all.'

Hipman had him. He was within his rights too. But Chiles might well be in the attack on Lucky Nugget. He had to be there. He compromised:

'OK, appoint me chief scout, acting and unpaid, and give me a sergeant who'll take my orders.'

'Raney.'

'He'll do. He gets the credit—'

'And you get Chiles. But save the town first. Your country comes before your vendetta.'

'I won't argue with you, sir. It'll come to the same thing anyway.'

Hipman stood up, walked over to a badly constructed cabinet and brought out a bottle and two glasses.

'I know you're not much of a drinker, Jack, but maybe you'd care to join me in a toast?'

Thorn nodded. Hipman handed him a glass. 'To victory!'

'Victory,' Thorn echoed, thinking that Custer probably drank the very same toast the night before his battle too.

FOUR

It was raining heavily as they left the fort. They were all drenched before they started, their capes and hats sodden. Thorn's borrowed cape brought back memories. But he was careful to let Raney lead within the fort. He'd had a word with him and found him compliant. Technically Hipman's instructions were illegal though it would be a foolish sergeant who held a major and fort commandant to the letter of the law, but Raney was actively happy with the idea. He preferred having an experienced 'officer' to give him orders, whether his commission was out of date or not.

Hipman stood by the gate seeing them off but he did no more than return their salutes. That was wise. Speeches were for politicians and even they were wise enough to avoid giving them in the rain.

'Maybe the weather'll put the Sioux off too,' Raney said as Thorn joined him outside the fort. 'They ain't exactly under orders like we are, they can always stay in their tepees.'

'We can't count on it,' Thorn said. 'And they're under orders in a different way. We all leave the army eventually. They never leave their tribe.'

Raney laughed briefly. 'What you're saying, sir, is that we can't count on them *not* coming.'

'Right, though out here call me "Jack".'

Raney nodded, adding: 'But not in town.'

'. . . "Sir" by itself doesn't make me a serving officer, it's just politeness, and as for "Captain" – well, I'm a retired captain. Courtesy again. I'll tell 'em I'm acting as chief scout, once.'

'It won't get Major Hipman into trouble?'

'Not if we succeed. If we don't, we'll be past caring and it won't matter much to him either.' He paused. 'You like him?'

'Like and respect him, Jack. He's a good officer. He ain't soft but he's fair. We all know he started as a ranker and made general in the war.'

'So did Custer,' Thorn said, 'made general, that is.'

'Yeah, I've heard tell of Autie. A good cavalryman but he lost a lot of men in the war. Hell, he led from the front but I reckon this time he'd just used up his luck.'

Thorn said nothing. Running down a brother officer before a sergeant wasn't what you learned to do at West Point. Still, it was as well to know. The rank and file were going to leave the crocodile tears to the boards of inquiry and the newspapers. Which didn't mean they wouldn't like some payback. Around 250 rankers had died alongside Custer.

'When do you reckon he'll hit us, sir?'

Thorn noticed the 'Jack' had been dispensed with.

'I doubt it'll be long,' he said. 'The Azats have been sitting on their backsides while the rest of the Sioux nation have been covering itself in glory by their standards. Our scalps would even the balance quite a bit.'

'We'd better disappoint 'em, then,' Raney said. 'I've always had a dread of going bald and doing it all at one go don't appeal at all!'

Thorn laughed. 'I doubt you'll get an argument with anyone on that, Raney,' he said. Ahead of them the western end of Lucky Nugget loomed in the rainy distance.

There were no cheering crowds as they rode in. Thorn got them under cover at the livery stables and left them there under Raney's watchful eye.

Letting them go on to the saloons would have been a sure way of dissolving the command almost instantly. He went in search of the mayor – Kefauver under another hat – and found him by his beloved safe along with Marshal Carey. It didn't take long to convince them that Lucky Nugget was in trouble.

'I'll get the word out,' Kefauver said. 'This place'll be awash with miners in a few hours. Most of 'em were soldiers during the war. Along with the troopers we'll give Zanai and his cut-throats a real shellacking!'

'No, not in the rain,' Thorn said. 'Think about it. Where are they going to wait?'

'In the saloons,' Marshal Carey put in.

'And what are they going to do there?'

The question hung in the air. The answer was obvious. They'd wait half an hour or so and, nothing having happened, they'd all have a drink. And still nothing having happened, another . . . and after a few more hours they'd go back to their respective workings with massive hangovers leaving the town even more vulnerable than it had been.

'We'll use the permanent townspeople,' Kefauver decided. 'With your permission, I'll contact a number of the steadier miners and have them ready to move in at an hour's notice.'

'Right,' Thorn said. 'I'll bring four of the soldiers here into the bank and have the rest set up in second-floor rooms. Townspeople with guns can do likewise. If you could arrange to keep them supplied with coffee and food, we'll be all right.'

'What about closing the town off?' Carey asked. 'You know, a few hidden wagons at either end of Main Street so that when the Sioux get here we can box 'em in.'

Thorn suppressed a sigh. It was a dime novel idea. Moving a wagon in the mud took manpower and when you were being shot at, the men tended to disappear. Besides which, they didn't know just how many hostiles there were going to be. If they came in force, they might need to drive them off rather than making a slugging match out of it, one they might not win. He explained, gently. Kefauver understood straight away. He'd make somebody a damn fine adjutant, Thorn thought.

'So what now?' Carey asked.

'We'll get everyone in position and wait,' Thorn said. As he said it he felt as if he really were back in the army though he absolutely wasn't, he knew. Neither Kefauver nor Carey had cared about his credentials beyond the fact that the soldiers were under his command. For them, it was a question of survival. For himself, it was that and something else. There was a chance that Zanai mightn't come in just with his braves. The gold in the bank safe was what Chiles was after. Maybe he'd be with them. It wasn't certain, maybe not even likely, but it just wasn't a chance Thorn could have forgone. Hipman had known that too.

Auguste was not best pleased to find himself amongst so many Indians. He had an uncomfortable feeling that once their blood was up they'd just see his yellow hair and develop a desire to wear it on their belts. But you didn't argue with Chiles, certainly not when gold was in question.

'Shouldn't we send out scouts?' he asked Zanai who was presently leading the party of forty braves hunkered down just three miles from town, presumably waiting for the rain to ease off.

'You see them, they see you,' Zanai said reasonably. 'Your job is Kefauver. Take him, no more.'

'Yeah,' Auguste said. They needed him alive. Maybe they could blow the safe but it was a dead certainty they could open it if they got hold of the bank manager. The Sioux could be very persuasive. Hell, so could he.

He looked up at the sky. Maybe the wait had been worthwhile. The rain would be letting up soon. There was blue sky moving in from the west. All the same, the town would be too wet to burn as originally intended. He almost sighed. There was nothing like leaving a burning town behind you to discourage pursuit.

He took out the butt of a cigar and lit it, cupping his hand over it to keep it dry in the rain, glancing around at the assembled Sioux. They didn't seem to mind the rain though they were as wet as he was . . . but they'd fight. He didn't need to know about Custer of the Seventh to know that. He could see it. He'd ridden on the Kansas Border and knew what real hardcases looked like and these were the real thing. Turning them loose on Yankees and Northerners didn't bother him either. The Yankees had employed Buffalo soldiers; this was a taste of their own medicine. But at bottom he was tired of it all. So was Chiles. The Old South was gone; the world was going in a different direction now, and he wanted his life back.

There was only one way to get it back – gold. God help any Yankee bastard who got in his way!

*

Thorn had expected they'd have to lie in wait for two or three days before the attack, not for any good reason but simply because in war you usually did. But the attack came late in the afternoon of the day they'd arrived. He'd had Raney set a lookout but they still had no more than a couple of minutes' warning – the Sioux were good at using the lie of the land to disguise their movements. Still, it was enough. He knew there were around forty or fifty of them along with one white man.

Chiles? He could hope at least. He passed the word, checked his six-gun and Winchester and waited with the four troopers in the bank. Aside from the soldiers spread through the town were men with long guns and six with shotguns, and that was pretty good odds, especially as they'd surprise on their side. Zanai wouldn't attack if he knew the town had been reinforced so he had to be expecting no more than minimal resistance. More than that, thinking he had surprise on his side, his discomfiture when finding he hadn't would be all the keener. . . .

Thorn cut himself short. Odds no longer mattered. Now it was time to fight and sometimes the odds didn't matter a damn anyway. He could be dead in a couple of minutes. He took position beside the trooper at the right front window, ready to smash the glass and fire as soon as a target presented itself – this town would be a glazier's paradise for the next week, if it survived. Nobody was going to open a window to fire, just use the butt end of a rifle to do the job.

He felt his heart beginning to pace in anticipation, forced himself to be calm. He'd fought enough battles, faced enough guns to know that fear was no protection at all. He glanced down at his hands. They were steady. He looked out of the window. Nothing yet.

'Captain, how do you reckon it, sir? I've never fought Indians afore.' The trooper beside him was looking to him. 'I was part of a draft sent three months back.'

'You were in the war?'

'No, sir, too young.'

Yes, he was, Thorn thought. It should have been obvious, except there was a battle pending and so nothing at all was obvious any more. 'Just keep down and shoot. Indians or Rebs, they can't harm you if you shoot 'em first.'

'Yes, sir.'

Was he relieved by that bit of advice? He

sounded to be but it didn't matter. When he got shot at he'd shoot back. Everybody did and usually missed too. But there'd be less of that than usual. The range would be very short indeed.

As always, the actual onset of the battle was very sudden. One moment the street was empty, the next it was full of men on horses firing into the buildings. They aimed low, at the ground-floor windows and even when they missed the thin boards of the buildings proved little obstacle. Unexpected, the onset would have been devastating but as Thorn had ordered everyone on to the upper storeys, it wasn't, and instead of a demoralized lack of response the Sioux in Main Street found themselves instantly under heavy fire.

Theoretically that first volley should have decimated them but Thorn saw only one man and one horse fall. First volleys often missed. Fear played a part and it wasn't easy to hit a moving target. But as in all battles it would be the last volley that decided everything.

But the Indians weren't interested in taking the town, just the bank, and several were dismounting before it. There had been no incoming fire into the bank itself though the troopers had already smashed the windows and started to fire out. Suddenly Thorn saw the man beside him crash back, a bullet through his temple. He fired himself – and then the dismounted Indians were in through the door. Hell, nobody had locked it! He briefly blamed himself and then forgot about it as an Indian fired at him with an ancient Paterson Colt .34 – and missed! He pulled the Winchester out of the window to return fire but the man was down already and he saw Kefauver standing in front of the safe as if to defend it, firing a small .32 pocket-pistol of some sort.

Thorn grinned – the damned fool hadn't realized he could defend it just as well from behind and have the advantage of its steel armour!

Suddenly he saw a white man amongst them. Just a glimpse of him. Chiles? He couldn't be sure but he surged up and moved into the moving mass of men, not shooting, just lashing out at them with the carbine in a wild attempt to get at the putative Chiles, only to see him pitch forward as Kefauver shot him with the last bullet in his puny but effective gun.

And then it was over inside the bank. The remaining Indians turned and fled to their horses and out in the street the shooting became less too.

Thorn stood over the fallen man, turned him over. He was quite dead, shot through the heart and he wasn't Chiles. No scar. And his hair was flaxen – Gus something or other.

Relief or regret? He wasn't sure. Reason told him one bullet would have been as good as another if it had been Chiles but a deep atavistic desire for it to be his bullet surged over him.

And then it was utterly quiet again. Deathly quiet. He looked around. Besides Gus there were two dead Sioux and the unfortunate trooper who'd shared the window with him. The rest were untouched, even the safe which Kefauver had foolishly protected with his own body.

He walked outside. There were several horses down and three Sioux lying dead in the dirt which seemed a small tally for the pandemonium of fire that there had been. As for the defenders' casualties, he couldn't tell but guessed they'd be low.

The raid had failed, failed miserably. Others realized it too and he heard an old sound, one he'd never heard on a battlefield before.

They were cheering.

Thorn took a deep breath. Let them, he thought, but he'd not join in. His plan had worked but, as he judged it, his leadership had been poor. He'd lost his temper and he could easily have got himself killed.

The thought of Chiles evading him was too much. He felt the bile rising in his throat, forced it down. He wasn't a shave-tail to be violently sick after a fire fight. Hell, what he needed was a drink. He started across the street for the nearest, now rather beat-up saloon.

Major William Hipman studied the two notes lying on his roughly made wooden desk. Raney's was brief. They had fought off and killed five Sioux and one renegade; a single trooper – O'Kelly – was dead, another wounded; several townspeople too, though none seriously. And that was it. He didn't use the word 'victory', merely providing a list.

Thorn's letter was entirely different. He mentioned light casualties on both sides and while he studiously avoided that same word he did give his opinion that Zanai would probably not try raiding Lucky Nugget again though he, Thorn, proposed keeping the half-troop there for the time being.

Hipman delved into a drawer, found a half-smoked cigar and lit it. No, he wasn't keeping them. Hipman knew his forces were simply too small even to consider dividing except under conditions of crisis. That had passed. Lucky Nugget's gold was safe from Zanai and that was all that interested him. Legally it should still be in the ground anyway. There were treaties with the Sioux to that effect though his lords and masters had told him not to enforce them.

Which was to the good as the miners might have given him a worse bloody nose than had Zanai. Morally, he didn't care. The truth was that the Sioux were brave and cruel but above all anachronistic. They needed hundreds of square miles to feed one village. They lived in the Stone Age and this was the Age of Steam.

He picked up Thorn's letter, tore it up and threw the fragments into the waste-bin. With nothing on paper Thorn's part in the petty victory no longer existed and couldn't embarrass the army. Raney's note he put in his filing-basket. That would cause no problems at all and would certainly make Raney's career. He'd end up a first sergeant. And Thorn wouldn't care about being ignored. All he really wanted was to find Chiles and that had eluded him. The messenger had confirmed that the renegade had straw-coloured hair.

So Chiles was at large and so were the rifles. They worried him a great deal. Not only Fort Burr was at stake, General Terry didn't need a major well-armed force to his rear, cutting his lines of communication. Custer's defeat might just be repeated. . . .

He picked up a pen and wrote to Raney. It was a very short note – '*Come back here.*' For Thorn he didn't even pen a note. Better nothing on paper. Hipman didn't really care about his career any more but he did care about due form. The army absolutely didn't need embarrassing at this time. So he'd send an oral message to the same effect and he'd mention Chiles. That would bring Thorn racing back without a doubt.

Thorn could be very useful indeed. Without further rifles the threat Zanai posed was containable. And Chiles was the key. Maybe Thorn could find that key for him.

A pity he had to use him like this. He liked the boy, always had, but it was a matter of duty. Besides, Thorn was just mad enough to do the impossible. He hoped so. He drew on his cigar and called out for the duty corporal.

Zanai watched young Hotad ride west; he had a pair of ponies and he would ride both to death to deliver his message to Sitting Bull, Crazy Horse and Little Cloud – not of victory, alas, but asking for their aid.

Had he been wrong joining the battle against

the Americans? When the news about Custer had reached his camp he had had little choice: either lead his men into the fight or find himself a leader without followers. And it was indisputable that the Americans were encroaching on the ancestral land. Once the Lakota and their allies had roamed the High Plains at will, following the buffalo for 1,000 miles and none had dared gainsay them – the Navaho had feared them, the Apache disappeared at their advent – they had truly been Lords of the West

And then in the space of a generation they had become supplicants for other men's food, living where they were told at the goodwill of men sent out to rule them, spied on by the hated Crow scouts from the fort, not the brave free men they had been but lousy reservation Indians.

No, the Azat could no longer live like that. Better to die with a lance in your hand and hatred in your belly. But those were just words and war was deeds. And guns.

Somehow he must still get those guns and for that he needed white man's money. Hotad's message might help there but nothing was certain.

He watched the rider as he disappeared over

the skyline, then looked back to the tepees of his village and lastly at the patch of dirt at his feet, still stained dark by Roman's blood.

It was fitting that he had been the first to die here, but in no way glorious. He had been no warrior, just an old man, easy to kill. Zanai looked over his village, its tepees sound, its people well-fed with white man's beef, and he felt a cold presentiment of disaster. Roman had once told him that in the great war the Americans had fought amongst themselves they had killed more of their own than there were people in all the tribes of the Indians of the Great Plains and, traitor though Roman might have been, that had been no lie, Zanai knew.

How could such might be defeated? It couldn't, but it wasn't here now. It was still concentrated in the East where the Americans lived and quick victories here might deter them from moving west – quick, total and bloody. They had to burn Fort Burr and leave not a soul alive.

He glanced back to the west and stared a moment at the empty horizon. Ride well, my son, he thought. We need those guns like life itself.

After a moment he went back inside his tepee,

his heart lighter than it had been. The path was chosen, there was no turning back, and it was an honourable path – the path of war.

FIVE

Jane watched the children troop out of the temporary schoolroom and started to wipe the blackboard. She had never imagined herself teaching school but it was better than the alternatives. Her father's death had left her destitute. Even the dress she was wearing was a gift from Mrs Raney; virtually her entire wardrobe came from a whip-round amongst the ladies of the fort.

They hadn't had a full-time teacher before, the better-educated of the ladies had been doing their best, and Major Hipman had even decided to pay her a very small salary – paid out of 'mess funds' he said but she rather suspected it was from his own pocket. But she would take it none the less. There was nothing else to do. Not that she'd stay here long. Once the emergency was over and it was safe to travel she'd get herself a job teaching in some town. As she hadn't even normal school credentials the job here would be a double help – she could cite it as experience.

Odd how her world had fallen apart in an afternoon, and how well she'd coped with it, much better than she would ever have expected to. She'd soon found out that weeping was no answer to anything and, besides, she liked teaching the kids.

There weren't many of them – most enlisted men didn't have families – and the standards expected weren't high, just reading, writing and ciphering. They'd scarcely been met, either. Mrs Raney and the other 'teachers' hadn't been dab hands at what they taught. Certainly the kids had been ignorant of the difference between an adverb and an adjective and as for long division it had been an arcane mystery.

No longer. She smiled to herself, thinking soon enough the kids might be regretting her presence. Her father had mostly educated her himself but she'd been a fair student and she could speak French just about, read Latin if she had to, and even had a hazy idea of the differential and the integral calculus. None of that would be called for here but later . . .

'Excuse me, ma'am.'

She turned, saw Thorn standing by the door, hat in hand.

'I'm sorry, school's finished for the day. What was it you wanted to learn – reading or ciphering?'

He smiled, relaxed a little, and she knew the little joke had served its purpose. The menfolk in the fort had all been afraid she might suddenly burst into tears at any moment. She'd found that the merest touch of humour set them at their ease. She said:

'My name's still Jane, by the way.'

'Jane,' he conceded.

'Except, that is, to my pupils. One must keep up the standards.' She put down the board rubber and went over to him as he was making no move to enter further himself.

'You seem to have settled in,' he said.

'Life goes on and I'm a professor's daughter, after all.'

He tensed a little at the mention of her father, she noticed. So had Major Hipman. So there was something they weren't telling her. Or maybe she was imagining it. 'Are you leaving?' she asked and found herself hoping the answer was no.

It was. 'I haven't anywhere to go for the moment. I don't think Hipman really needs a chief scout any longer but he says he does.'

'You're hoping for news of Chiles,' she said.

Thorn nodded. 'Though I expect he's long gone by now.'

'Maybe not. From what Major Hipman said, he was after money. He didn't get it, and he still has the guns.'

'He mentioned them?'

'He wondered if I could help – if they'd been smuggled into the agency.' She paused. 'I was able to give him a definite no. I did all the ordering and checked deliveries. My father was an able mathematician but he was a poor bookkeeper.'

Thorn said nothing.

'So if you're right about Chiles having several hundred guns to sell he brought them in as farm or ranch goods. He has an accomplice . . .' And suddenly she knew. How careful Hipman had been with his questions. How careful Thorn was now. The 'why' was obvious. Her father had been the author of his own misfortune, he'd been a . . .

She didn't finish the sentence even in the privacy of her mind. Tears, she found after all, did have a purpose.

'I'm fine now,' she said, adding a little ungenerously: 'don't fuss.'

Thorn said nothing, glad at least the weeping

had been of such brief duration. It was some-thing beyond his competences.

'You never were going to tell me, were you – both you and Hipman?'

So she'd guessed.

'What good could it do to know your father was . . .' He broke off.

'A traitor?' She shook her head. 'You're both too much soldiers still. At least Major Hipman has good excuse for it but you've got your own private continuation war.' She paused. 'My father wasn't betraying anybody, at least by his lights. Don't you see, he was a criminal! He was in it for the money. And I guess Chiles's attitude is just the same. Maybe always was.

'You were thinking Dad got kicked out for being a Southern sympathizer and came here burning for vengeance.' She shook her head. 'He got kicked out, true, but that was a different kind of politics, *college* politics!

'Oh, he'd been against the war but that was because he thought it foolish and immoral, conscripting boys in the North for cannon fodder . . . but so did the new dean. Dad had been up for the job too and failed to get it. Thereafter Dean Cosgrove did everything he could to drive him out and eventually succeeded – because they'd hated each other for twenty years, all over a review written by my father of Cosgrove's book.' She shook her head. 'He was a brilliant man but just for once he was stupid.' She paused, then: 'And maybe he did it for me . . .'

'Maybe,' Thorn conceded, 'but it's not your fault whatever the reason and there are fools who'd blame you too.'

She smiled at him. 'Thank you for that. But it doesn't change anything for you, does it?'

'No.'

'Chiles is almost a phantom, Jack. He's not the *guerrillero* he once was. He's just a thief looking for a fast buck. He's spent money on those rifles. He'll want it back. There's one thing thieves can't abide – having things stolen from them. And that's how he'll see it.' She shook her head. 'Does that help any?'

'It just might, Jane,' Thorn said. 'I'm much obliged.'

Outside, Thorn paused to light a cigar. A remarkable girl, Jane – quick, intelligent and handsome too. His late wife Elise had been . . .

He cut the thought off. What was the use in making comparisons? Or even thinking about Jane at all? He'd work to do. If she were right, Chiles wouldn't do the sensible thing and disappear, he'd keep trying to sell the guns.

And Thorn couldn't see any other likely buyer but Zanai. So the guns stayed in place and if he could find them, he'd find Chiles. Jane had said Roman had had nothing to do with bringing them in. That was true, he trusted her implicitly. So who had? It had to be—

'Sir?'

Thorn looked up. A soldier was standing before him.

'Major Hipman's compliments, sir and he'd like to see you at your earliest convenience.'

Thorn laughed. 'Like now?'

'I guess so, sir.'

He glanced regretfully back at the closed door, then:

'Lead on, trooper.'

MAJOR HIPMAN OFFICER COMMANDING FORT BURR STOP LITTLE CLOUD RIDING EAST VIA CANADA GAP STOP OVER 300 HOSTILES STOP HOLD FORT BURR AT ALL COSTS STOP GENERAL TERRY STOP

Thorn put the telegram on the desk. 'So the telegraph is working again,' he said.

'Not quite,' Hipman replied. 'A rider brought that half an hour ago from Johnson's Rift, to the south. There's a cavalry detachment there.'

'Well, at least the good general doesn't ask you to go out and defeat them.'

'He could as well have,' Hipman said. 'Reckon on half being armed with guns and suppose Zanai has about fifty rifles as of now. That's odds of three to one. It's not good but I can hold out. But if Zanai gets the rest of the guns then the odds are nearly ten to one. A few timber palisades won't keep them out.'

'But Zanai doesn't have the gold.'

'Maybe he'll have something nearly as good. Maybe Little Cloud is bringing it with him.'

Thorn looked a question.

'There were two telegrams. The other's in code, officers only. Not even chief scouts can see it.' He paused. 'But possibly the Sioux took a paymaster's wagon not long back, just after the Custer débâcle. Or not: I'm just speculating, you understand.'

Like Hell! Thorn thought. 'It's a free country so they say. I reckon you can do that.'

'I might even speculate that after Lucky Nugget Zanai sent out a rider and asked for help. The Sioux have little use for treasury bills but they have for guns and allies.'

'So by saving Lucky Nugget we didn't save the situation, we just made it worse. Little Cloud wouldn't be coming otherwise.'

'It's possible. And the truth is, there isn't a damned thing I can do to stop him. Canada Gap is flat land to the north of the plateau. If I tried to head him off my "troop' would be massacred, the fort would fall and the town after it.'

'So I need to find Chiles.'

'The devil with Chiles!' Hipman snapped. 'Find the guns. If you get Chiles while doing it, all to the good, but we've just lost a regiment. A fort would be too much.'

Which was true. In the long run it wouldn't matter. The Sioux were doomed by their success. More of it would just up the payback, but in the short run . . .

'I've just been talking to Jane,' Thorn said. 'She said you had too.'

'I did,' Hipman said, somewhat defensively, Thorn thought. He considered telling him she knew the whole of it, decided against. 'The upshot is that we worked out Chiles had to have local help.'

Hipman nodded. 'A rancher, I'd guess.'

'But which?'

Hipman smiled. 'That's what you're getting the big bucks for.'

Eighty a month if he were taking it, which he wasn't. But it was a sight better than a private's pay and there was a good chance that they wouldn't live even to collect that.

'Terry didn't happen to mention a relief force in that secret telegram of his, did he?' Thorn asked.

'No,' Hipman said. 'We're on our own.'

Kefauver scratched his chin dubiously.

'I'm not sure I can help you, Captain Thorn. It's a matter of banking confidentiality.'

Thorn glanced pointedly at the window where the soldier had died.

'We're at war, Kefauver. If one of your customers is in league with the Sioux, he's the one subverting confidentiality. And committing treason.' Whether that was legally true he had no idea but no doubt a case could be made for it. 'I recall you standing before that safe bravely defending your bank and its assets. This is no different.'

Kefauver smiled suddenly. 'That wasn't brave, believe me. I just lost my temper. If I'd thought about it, I'd have stood behind the safe.' He paused. 'I didn't sleep well that night and that's a fact!'

Thorn took out the copy of the open telegram Hipman had had copied for him.

'Read that.'

Kefauver did so, then: 'Is this true?'

'Ask General Terry. He sent it,' Thorn said conclusively. He took the copy back from Kefauver, now looking very unsure, and pressed home his advantage. 'I don't want to go over your books personally, Kefauver. I'm pretty sure I wouldn't understand 'em, not being a banker, but I do need to know who brought that consignment of guns in. It wouldn't be set down as guns but as ranching equipment or . . .' He gestured, openly. 'Obviously I don't know, but if you think about it, I reckon you might.'

Kefauver was wavering. Thorn just waited. Let him convince himself. Suddenly Kefauver went from his desk to the door and locked it, turned the sign to closed. 'We can leave by the back way. It's convenient for my house. If you'd care to accompany me . . .'

Thorn noticed that he was taking no books with him; presumably he had no need; it was all in his head.

'Why not?'

'Will you take tea, Captain Thorn?' Mrs Kefauver asked. She was in her thirties, decorously rather than expensively dressed, and handsome rather than pretty. 'Or would you prefer coffee?'

'Tea would be fine, Mrs Kefauver,' he said; for

all he detested the stuff, this was the time to make accommodations.

'Go with your mother, Harry,' Kefauver said to his only son, an eight-year-old boy with large blue eyes that had been fixed on Thorn ever since he had entered the modest house just behind the bank. Thorn now nodded to him in a friendly fashion but, probably out of shyness, the boy didn't respond except by disappearing into the kitchen.

'He's a good lad,' Kefauver said. 'I only wish there were a decent school for him. His mother tutors him now. She went to normal school herself.'

'Yes,' Thorn said, noticing how cluttered the room was with china ornaments, tables, pictures on the wall. The price of domesticity.

'I—' Kefauver began only to be interrupted by the advent of his wife bearing a tea-tray. She set this down on a nearby table, poured out two cups. Thorn assured her he took it without milk or sugar – Kefauver took both – and was given a cup and saucer and a plate of cookies.

'I'll leave you to your talk,' she said smiling. 'I hope you enjoy the cookies.'

Kefauver smiled at her as she left.

'Well?'

'I don't know—' Kefauver began.

'I think you do,' Thorn interrupted, setting saucer and plate on a nearby table, rather precariously for there was little room left on it. 'Imagine what the Sioux would do to your wife and son, your house, your bank. I saw Roman die, his house burn. They won't worry about banking regulations, believe me.' It came out a touch stronger than intended but from the look on Kefauver's face he saw it had worked.

'Very well,' said the banker after a moment, 'you've made your point. There were two consignments in the last six months that could have been the guns – I'm assuming the guns would have made two wagon loads?'

'Yes,' Thorn agreed.

'Then it's either the Tranter ranch to the east or the Dogget ranch to the south. I handled the payments for both.'

'Tell me about Tranter.'

'He's about my age. He's got both cattle and horses.'

'What kind of man is he?'

'A good man. The consignment was for a tin roof for his barn.'

'And does his barn have a new roof?'

Kefauver nodded.

'What about Dogget then?'

'Mr Dogget's an old man. He has two sons—'

'Who don't get on?'

Kefauver looked at him suspiciously. 'How do you know?'

'I don't. What was the consignment?'

'Drilling equipment for wells.'

'Have they a new well?'

'I can't say.'

'I'm obliged, Kefauver,' Thorn said. There was no point in pressing him further. He could find out the rest in the nearest saloon without embarrassing the banker. Why he should care, he wasn't sure. Perhaps the image of him defending his livelihood and honour in front of that safe, or maybe his domestic situation, Thorn wasn't sure. He stood up. 'Thank Mrs Kefauver for me, would you? Fine tea.'

'But—' Kefauver stopped himself, realizing that, courtesy aside, the departure of his guest was now exactly what he wanted. 'I hope I've helped.'

'So do I, Kefauver – for all our sakes.'

It took no more than an hour and several rounds of drinks to learn the Dogget family history. It had been the first horse ranch in the region; old Kyle Dogget, the father, had been the first to trade with the Indians too, but only horses. There was no hint he'd ever sold guns nor did Thorn suspect him now. But, as he had suggested, the two sons, Angus and Donald, were at daggers drawn. There'd once been a fist fight between the two, outside the Bella Union. Marshal Carey had stopped it before any real damage had been done and given the pair a lecture on the lines of look what happened between Cain and Abel, which may have worked though the general opinion was that the Greener shotgun he'd been holding at the time had been more persuasive. There'd been little overt trouble since but it gave Thorn reason to believe he'd found Chiles's accomplices – the brother who wouldn't inherit. To know which he'd need to see Kyle Dogget's will and as Lucky Nugget didn't currently have an attorney that would be lodged in the bank. He knew Kefauver couldn't be pushed that far and it didn't matter. It wasn't his job to make a legal case, just to find the guns. And with them, Chiles.

The hatred was very cold now, had been for years. There would be no pleasure in killing him or handing him over to be hanged, and little satisfaction either. It was pure necessity, no less and no more. Afterwards, he'd go home and . . .

And what? Settle down like Kefauver into cosy domesticity? Maybe. It seemed inconceivable at the moment; no doubt it had been so to Kefauver once, but there he was, amidst tea, cookies and clutter, and thriving on it.

Such were his thoughts as he rode south towards the Dogget ranch.

'From New Mexico, eh?' Kyle Dogget said, leaning back in his imported armchair. 'Can't see why you'd be interested in horse-raising in these parts. Can't see how a man can be in two places at once, eh?' And he laughed, an old man's laugh, verging on a cackle.

'You're quite right, sir,' Thorn said. He was sitting opposite the old man alongside the elder brother, Angus. 'I'd have to employ a foreman to run it, but once the railroads open up this country the Chicago market will be fully open to you and there's the Canadian market too.'

'Canada? We don't sell to Canada! Raise their own in Canada.' Suddenly a touch of avarice could be heard in the old man's voice as he added: 'Still, land's cheap around here. A wise man might do well to buy, and having land, what do you do with it? You raise stock. You've got your head screwed on, young feller, no doubt of it. And our stock is as good as you'll find in these parts. Set you up fine, it would.'

'I'm just making preliminary enquiries for the

moment,' Thorn said. 'I've other business here but—'

'Chief scout for the army,' Angus put in.

'Temporarily,' Thorn said, 'and as a favour to Major Hipman. I served with him during the war. Once this Sioux business is settled—'

'Can't understand that,' Kyle Dogget broke in. 'Never had any trouble with Zanai. Sensible feller, a good judge of horseflesh too. Can't think why there was that trouble in town. Probably all the fault of those miners. I never trust a man who's out for gold. He'll kill you as soon as look at you. Easy money, that's all they're after. Dig it up and away to some city and spend it on whores and liquor. Not honest work at all.' He shook his head. 'I never had any trouble with Zanai. Knew his father, Little Feather, the old chief. A fine man. He was old then, as old as I am now, I reckon. But no trouble at all. We kept off the plateau but we traded – horses for their fine pelts. They raised their own horses too but mustang stock. Knew a good horse when he saw one did Little Feather.' He paused and then added somewhat querulously: 'Can't see why there's all this trouble. Always trouble . . .'

Angus stood up. 'I'll show you around, Mr Thorn.'

Thorn stood up too. 'I'll take my leave of you,

sir,' he said to the old man who he now realized was, if not quite senile, headed that way. And Angus knew it too.

'Good luck, young feller. Buy land by all means. Always a good investment. Good day to you.'

'He gets tired very easily,' Angus Dogget said when they were outside. It was virtually a defence of his father's sanity.

Thorn merely nodded. After a moment he said:

'I didn't mention it earlier but I'm also interested in existing ranches.'

Angus Dogget's mouth hardened. 'This ranch is not for sale.'

'Of course,' Thorn said, very reasonably, 'not yours, but other ranches go out of business, land comes on the market. I might be able to use a partner for acquiring such. Let me establish my bona fides.' He showed Angus his letter of credit. It obviously impressed him. 'You could always contact me through Mr Kefauver at the bank. No promises but . . .' He let the sentence hang, feeling no guilt at all about tricking the man. He might even be saving his life.

'I'll bear it in mind.'

'I hear you're into well-digging at the moment.'

'Wells?' Angus Dogget shook is head. 'We have one for the house —' he gestured at it— 'but the land itself is well watered. We've several streams for the horses.'

'I must have got it wrong,' Thorn said, suppressing as best he could a feeling of triumph as he added, 'unless your brother is—'

'Donald's my younger brother,' Angus said coldly. 'He sees to the ponies on the north-eastern range. That's well-watered too.'

'I rode in from the north but I never saw him or the ponies.'

'You wouldn't. It's two miles due east of the trail, in the hills. Not the best grazing but good enough for ponies. And my brother' – he didn't say it but it was in his tone. 'You know Donald?'

Thorn shook his head. 'I just heard the ranch was run by two brothers.'

'No, it's run by me,' Angus said forcefully. 'Donald just helps out.'

Thorn could feel it; he was on the verge! He rode north slowly, wondering whether to go back to the fort for a few soldiers, dismissed the idea. He might miss Chiles that way.

He glanced at the sun. Another two hours before nightfall. Why not use the night? He doubted he'd find anything in the dark but he'd

be on the spot when morning came and when
Donald Dogget, hearing they'd had an inquisitive visitor, would do what came naturally. His
first thought would be for the guns and his
second to check on them. He might even have
Chiles with him for that. All Thorn would have
to do would be to lie doggo and watch.

With cold anticipation he turned east.

It was two hours off nightfall and all day Little
Cloud and Zanai had been talking, snarling at
each other more like, and it wasn't just down to
the north Lakota language. They didn't like
each other. Which was just as well, Chiles
thought; when Little Cloud had first seen him in
the village there had been death in his eyes.
Nothing personal, he guessed; the young chief
felt like that about all whites.

A brave prodded him, pointed. Chiles understood. He was being summoned to the tepee
itself. To have his throat cut? Possible though
unlikely but better perhaps than dying under
the gun of that madman Thorn who'd chased
after him all these years. He entered the tepee to
see Little Cloud and Zanai seated cross-legged
across from each other, a leather bag between
them. He sat without waiting for an invitation,
nearer Zanai than Little Cloud.

'Tell Little Cloud about the guns,' Zanai said.

'He speaks English?' Chiles asked, surprised.

Neither replied which could only be an affirmation.

'There are four hundred and seventy-five of them, just like the ones you've seen, and a supply of percussion caps, fifty per gun.'

'Powder?' Little Cloud asked.

'A very little.'

'No matter, we have powder,' Little Cloud said, his English surprisingly good. 'Bring them here.'

'For gold,' Chiles said.

'No gold.'

'Then no guns.' Weakness would get his throat cut quicker than anything else, he was sure.

Little Cloud picked up the leather satchel, threw it to him. Chiles examined it. The outside was stamped: 'US Govmt.' He opened it. Paper – paper money! A stolen paymaster's satchel. He estimated there were $10,000 there all told.

'It's less than we agreed,' he said, looking to Zanai who said nothing. Chiles shrugged. 'Why not? The guns were made for my people, to kill bluecoats with. It's fitting they do that.'

'You are enemy to the bluecoats?' Little Cloud asked.

Chiles nodded and Zanai said something in Lakota, presumably confirming it. He'd explained the war at some length to him, suspecting the Sioux had no taste for traitors, whatever agreements they made with them. As was demonstrated by what had happened to Roman.

'Why?'

The simplicity of the question took Chiles by surprise. How could he explain to a man who scarcely knew what a state was, let alone the rights accruing to it? He said: 'They wanted to take away our slaves.'

Little Cloud looked hard at him and then suddenly the tension was diminished. They had reached some kind of understanding. The Sioux had few slaves, their wandering life style precluded it, but he wouldn't give up any his tribe had because someone told him to.

'The guns,' Little Cloud said.

Chiles stood up. 'I'll get them now.' He bent to pick up the money.

'No, come back here, then get it.'

Chiles shook his head. He looked to Zanai.

'Give me three warriors and four horses. They can bring the wagons back here. And give one of your men the money. When he sees the guns, he gives me the money.'

'No trust us?' Little Cloud asked, smiling ferally.

'No more than I have to.'

Little Cloud looked to Zanai who gestured affirmatively. He turned back to Chiles.

'You get men, horses, money if speak truth. No harm come to you. If you lie—'

'I'm not lying,' Chiles said. 'Ask Zanai. I have not lied to him. And I'd not lie to a man who fought and killed Custer – my enemy too. I thank you for it.'

'No need, not done for you.'

'Nevertheless . . .'

'Go to guns, you get money. Never come back. I see you, I kill.' And suddenly Little Cloud smile showing a perfect set of slightly yellowing teeth. Chiles smiled back. The Sioux was a man after his own heart.

There were four main hills, not very high but tangled with vegetation. Thorn had arrived too near nightfall and all his plans for further investigation had come to naught. Blundering about in the dark would have only earned him a fall or an injury so he'd cached himself and his horse a few feet into the tangle and made a cold camp.

And now he could see the early-morning light through the leaves and he realized he'd slept

better than he had for years. He shrugged off
the blanket, stood up, batted himself down.
He'd slept with his six-gun in its holster so his
dressing was completed by stooping to pick up
his hat which had served in the office of a pillow,
much to its detriment.

Today I will see Chiles, he told himself, and
then he set the matter aside. That didn't need
any more thought. Oddly, he found himself
thinking about Jane. Her day would be beginning too. No home, no servant now, nothing but
a charity job teaching children for a pittance.
Maybe her father had deserved what he got, she
hadn't.

He shook his head, found some pemmican in
his saddlebag and chewed on that for breakfast.
His first job was to find a suitable place, then
watch. He'd done the like before, many times,
and he knew it was better to keep your mind
empty, concentrated solely on the sights and
sounds round about – like a cat watching for its
prey.

Donald Dogget was an inch shorter than his
brother and a year younger. Aside from that they
were hard to tell apart in looks or character.
Both were acquisitive, a touch on the ungener-
ous side, quick to find fault and a trifle cold-

hearted. Even the inch difference in height was negated by the fact that Donald had the heels of his boots built high. But he couldn't make himself a year older and he was sure his father would leave the ranch to the elder because that was exactly what he would do himself. So when Chiles had asked him for a private place to store two wagons full of guns, he'd agreed. Gold was an adequate substitute for land. Besides, at that time trading guns to the Indians would only have got him banned from the territory. Now, after Custer, the rope was almost certain.

He shuddered, looked behind him but he saw no one, certainly not Thorn on the eastern hill, for Thorn was well back in the tangle of vegetation, even his carbine held low in the shade to avoid any glinting in the sun.

Dogget rode up the middle hill, following the old slippage line which wasn't at all obvious till you walked the land as he had when a boy. It was also wide enough for a wagon. Halfway up, out of sight of the eastern hill now, he slowed up, seeing fresh marks on the trail – horses, not wagons. As it was only lightly grassed talus it was easy to read sign. This was just Chiles, he decided after a moment. He checked on the guns fairly often. He was not a trusting man.

At last he reached the top and saw the wagons

in the dip below – but they were being harnessed up by Chiles and three Sioux braves, and using ponies too. They'd do the job but it would wind them for life.

'Charlie,' he began, staying his horse. Charlie Chiles looked up, saw him, drew and shot him in the face.

Thorn was just starting up the trail when he heard the shot. He dismounted immediately, led his horse into the trees just off the trail, hitched it to a low branch and, taking the carbine and its sheath, continued up on foot, keeping to the edge of the trail this time so he could slip unseen into the tangle of trees and bushes if need be.

There was no need. They were still harnessing the loaded wagons when he reached the top – three Sioux warriors and Chiles. Donald Dogget lay beside his horse, very dead. Thorn wasn't in the least surprised. Dogget had been a fool to think Chiles would keep any bargain he didn't have to.

He knelt down there in the bushes, watching, setting his hatred aside now. He couldn't afford it. The odds were four to one but he had surprise on his side. And the terrain too. The hilltop sank well down into a dip and that was where the wagons were. But the only way out was past him. He had them hemmed in.

He got down on his belly, aimed his carbine, centring on Chiles. The temptation to ease the trigger back was almost overwhelming but he had to think. Stopping the guns getting to the Sioux was the most important thing. It could mean thousands dead otherwise.

His own vengeance had to come second to that. He noticed that the nearer wagon was already harnessed up. Drop the lead horse, making it impossible to move and blocking the other too?

He calculated as coldly as he could manage. The risk was too great. He needed to cut down the odds and that first surprise shot was a certainty. He'd have a second chance with the wagon horse. And Chiles was the obvious candidate. He was wearing a six-gun and had a repeating carbine in one hand. The Indians had one-shot caplock rifles.

But that was exactly what he wanted. Was he weighing the odds?

No. And then Chiles started towards the nearer wagon. Thorn centred on his chest. Head shots were usually fated but the bigger target was more certain. He started to pull back the trigger, gently. And then one of the Indians spoke, Chiles turned. . . .

Crack!

Chiles was batted away and sent tumbling but Thorn knew instantly that he hadn't got him dead centre. Yet there was no time for self-recrimination. He worked the lever, shot the lead horse on the nearer wagon. It crumpled. The Sioux were going for their guns but unsure still where the shots were coming from. He shot one in the chest, saw him fall. The tall Sioux with the single feather in his headband had worked out where he was, thrown down some kind of pouch he was holding, found his gun and fired. He heard the shot but the bullet came nowhere near him. Thorn fired back, the man fell.

Two to one and the chances were that Chiles was badly hurt. Maybe. It was only a pistol bullet the Winchester fired. If he'd hit him with a Springfield military ball he'd be *hors de combat* for certain. If one of those hit your leg, you usually lost it; and often enough, your life. And surprise was gone too. They were both hunkered down behind the far wagon and boxes of rifles made for excellent armour. He had the advantage of height but that was all. And now they had to know where he lay.

He edged to the left, watching all the time. A bullet slammed into the vegetation not very far from where he'd been lying. But he'd seen the barrel flash briefly in the sun. Whoever it was he was on the right of the wagon. Thorn fired back with no obvious result. He fired again and again. No luck.

Suddenly the last Indian was on his feet and running for a still unharnessed horse, weaving as he did so. Realizing he needed to reload soon, Thorn conserved his shot. The Indian had to ride towards him and then he'd be an easy target.

Except he didn't. Keeping low on his horse he went straight up the banked side of the dip, through bushes and tangled vegetation. For a second Thorn was too surprised to react, then, as he reached the top, the Indian straightened up for an instant and Thorn fired, saw him shudder but not fall off, and then rider and mount were over the edge and lost to sight.

It would be good to think he wouldn't make it but Thorn knew he couldn't assume it. Rather, he had to assume that he would and soon enough he'd bring more Sioux back for the guns. Which meant they had to be destroyed here and quickly.

Except Chiles was down there with a repeating carbine, wounded but active. A stand-off but for the fact that Chiles might have allies on the way while he could expect none.

I had him in my sights! he accused himself, and rejected the charge instantly. The movement had been unexpected, unpredictable. In war, and this had been war *en petit*, nothing went exactly to plan. The thing to do was to get him to make a mistake, and there was nothing like bullets singing and ricocheting around you for that. He set the carbine down and began extracting bullets from his gunbelt to fill the magazine, thinking how convenient it was that the Winchester accepted the same bullets as his six-gun.

It was at that precise moment that Chiles made his move, coming out from behind the wagon to where the dead Sioux with the solitary feather now lay, not for the Indian's sake but to grab the leather satchel lying nearby.

Thorn snatched up the Winchester, aimed, fired, and the bullet spattered Chiles with dirt. Chiles turned, leaving the satchel, and ran for his horse. Thorn could see the blood on his shirt. A shoulder wound, painful but not disabling.

No mistakes this time, he thought, aiming for the head as Chiles mounted, a perfect target. He worked the lever automatically. . . .

Click.

The carbine was empty. There was no time to

reload. He cast it aside and drew his six-gun. Come this way! he half-prayed but Chiles had seen the Sioux escape over the rim and not only did he follow his example, he made for the edge furthest from Thorn.

Wounded or not, Chiles was fully the equal of the Sioux as a horseman. Horse and rider made it up the difficult, obstructed slope at speed. There were some sixty yards now between them. Thorn fired shot after shot, hoping. But both horse and rider made it to the top untouched and then the revolver clicked on an empty chamber. And Chiles was gone.

Thorn sat on the ground for a while, leaning forward as if in pain. Then he took a deep breath. He'd done the right thing. Chiles would wait. He'd waited all these years. The important thing was the guns. He'd done most of his duty there. Now was the time to do the rest. He found the carbine and began refilling it. After that, the six-gun and then he would go down into the killing-field.

They were all quite dead – Dogget and the two Sioux. He found that the satchel Chiles had tried for contained cash, presumably payment for the guns. That pleased him a little. A man without financial resources was limited in his actions. Besides, logic told him where Chiles was going. He had to have guessed who'd shot him – a single man, so himself. He would expect to be chased so he would continue in the direction he'd started, north. He wouldn't risk doubling back because he would expect to be instantly pursued. He wouldn't forgo any vengeance of his out of duty and would assume the like of others.

Thorn examined the guns, well over 400 he estimated. They were all like the one he'd seen in Zanai's village, good quality Reb work, probably bought for a song. There was just a small package of powder but there was a whole case of caps, on the old side now but effective, no doubt. He guessed there would be ball ammunition somewhere but he didn't search it out.

So how did he destroy them? The powder would blow up a few but only a few. He could always move them but you can't hide wagon ruts easily. Tipping the wagons down the hill? That would be hard and wouldn't serve. They were tough wagons. In effect, he'd just be making it easier for the Indians to get at them.

So it had to be fire. He freed the ponies, drove them off, smashed the cases open and flung caps all over them. That should keep the blaze going. Then he found the axle-grease containers under both wagons, spread the contents liberally and threw in the powder too. Two lighted lucifers completed the job and the wagons started hissing away splendidly, crackling like spit on a hob from the caps. He guessed the fires wouldn't totally destroy the rifles but the wooden furniture would be gone and most of the barrels askew. Useless for non-mechanically minded Indians.

He picked up the satchel of money but left the bodies – no time for the usual decencies – and walked all the way up to the rim before looking back.

The wagons were burning and cackling away better than he'd anticipated. And suddenly it occurred to him what the gunpowder was for – to blow up the caps if need be. Without them the guns would have been useless anyway

He laughed to himself. Whatever, he'd done the right thing. He stared at the twin pyres – not only of Chiles's hopes but of the Sioux's chance of ultimate victory. He had done his duty to his country if not to himself.

He turned and walked slowly down the trail to reclaim his horse and restart his seemingly eternal pursuit of Charlie Chiles.

SIX

Hipman seemed to have aged ten years since he'd last seen him. He hadn't slept, that was obvious, and neither had many in the fort. On the way in Thorn had seen troopers making small mines, Raney supervising, and the walls had double the usual number of sentries. He delivered the news without delay:

'The guns are destroyed.'

Hipman let out a breath, but it wasn't the relief of a man who'd been reprieved, more that of a man who'd been told his sentence had been commuted from hanging, drawing and quartering to simple beheading. Thorn followed up with the facts, briefly.

'Thanks, Jack,' Hipman said when he'd finished. 'I'm sorry about Chiles but you did your whole duty. Consider yourself discharged as chief scout. Take the girl and leave, and do it quickly.'

He meant it, Thorn saw. Hipman thought he was going to lose the fort despite the mines and the lost guns.

'How many men did Little Cloud bring?'

'Well over three hundred.'

'How armed, sir?'

'According to my Crow scouts, every brave seemed to have a gun.' Hipman paused. 'I know the fort's walls give us an advantage, supposedly ten to one, but I lost men last night on those walls. Arrows. Some emboldened Sioux crept close up and I've two men less today.' He shook his head. 'They could wear us down but they won't. Being here in such force means Little Cloud will be joined by all of Zanai's men, guns or not. And only half my men are really effective. Remember, the Sioux took on a full regiment of cavalry, killed half and drove the rest off. They're on a roll, Jack. All they need to do is attack *en masse* and we're lost. Once inside the fort, a lance and a knife will be just as deadly as a gun.'

Thorn was silent a moment. Hipman thought he was going to die and he couldn't fault his logic. Without artillery, without promise of relief, the chances were that Hipman was right.

The temptation for Thorn was to say that he'd

stay anyway but he held back. Hipman had just discharged him from his rather spurious duties. He wasn't in the army any longer and he'd no duty to die in this forlorn place for no good reason. In fact, if he were certain the fort was doomed, he would leave. There was always Chiles . . .

And then he recalled he'd still one more duty to perform. He handed over the satchel.

'There's around ten thousand dollars there, sir. I haven't counted it. I reckon it's from some payroll taken by the Sioux.'

Hipman didn't even open it. What was money, even in spectacular moments, in these circumstances?

Thorn waited for the children to leave before he entered the schoolroom. Her face brightened when she saw him.

'I heard you were back,' she said, smiling restrainedly at him.

How lovely she was, he noticed as if for the first time. There she stood, in a dowdy dress with chalk marks on it, in a storeroom in a doomed fort, and he felt an immense desire to protect her, to pluck her out of this place, to take her to safety.

'Is Chiles—'

'He has my lead in him,' Thorn said, rather brutally, 'but he's alive and kicking.'

She said nothing.

'The guns are destroyed,' he added, more softly.

She let out a breath. 'Then you've righted my father's wrong,' she said. 'I'm grateful.'

And it struck him that he'd done exactly that. The books now balanced.

He said: 'It had nothing to do with you, Jane, but as you say, it's wiped away. It never happened.'

'You really mean that?'

'I do,' he said with conviction. He added: 'There's one more thing. I want you to leave—'

'No.'

'I've just talked to Hipman. The fort's more than likely going to fall and—'

'Are you leaving?'

He hesitated. He hadn't thought it through but, forced to choose, he shook his head. He couldn't desert, scuttle away and leave his friend to perish along with his command. It was the rational thing to do but he just couldn't bring himself to do it, not even for revenge.

'Then I'm staying too.'

Thorn smiled at her, despite himself. There had been no defiance or arrogance in her words, just determination. Still, he tried to argue.

'You can do no good—'

'I'm employed here. I'm the schoolteacher. I can't leave my pupils.'

And put like that he couldn't argue against it.

'You have my respect, ma'am,' he said, suddenly formal.

She understood. 'Is there no hope at all?'

He shook his head. 'If they attack, and everything suggests they will, there'll be too many of them to hold off. The fort just won't be defensible.'

'So why not attack them?' she asked and then, realizing, put her hand to her mouth. 'I'm sorry, I'd no right to say that. I—'

But Thorn gestured the apology away, an idea burgeoning in his mind.

Then: 'I'm glad you did say it. Just maybe you could have saved all our lives.'

'You're mad,' Hipman said bluntly.

'Very probably, but hear me out anyway,' Thorn replied, unabashed, and went on to detail the plan that had grown in his mind since coming from the schoolroom and which he now presented to the man who would have to carry it out. He concluded by adding: 'Miss Roman prompted me to think of it, sir. She asked a simple question – If a defence is doomed, why not attack?'

'A pearl of strategic wisdom,' Hipman commented acidly. Then: 'A lovely girl that, father be damned.'

'And?'

'I've already told you, it's mad. But it might just work. Whatever, it's better than just waiting to get our throats cut.'

'It'll work, sir.'

Hipman smiled suddenly. 'You believe, don't you, son? You can't die here while Chiles lives.' He paused. 'Maybe you're right. I don't know why vengeance should let you lead a charmed life but maybe it does at that. Yet if you do survive, finish him quick and start living your own life. You're a rich man with good lands in New Mexico. Find yourself a good woman and grab a bit of happiness before you're too damned old.'

'Yes, sir,' Thorn said, a little amazed. Hipman wasn't given to issuing such advice.

'Now, I believe we've another battle to win, Captain.'

'That we do, General,' Thorn replied.

All the Sioux needed to do to win the battle was to attack that day. Thorn took over the supervision of the mines and their fuses as the latter had now to be modified. He had them re-cut and connected up in series for ease of igniting. That was easy enough. The junctions were ensured by a pinch of powder, bound in and sealed in pitch to keep the powder dry when it was buried in the earth. The quickmatch itself was pre-soaked in nitrate of potassium so it didn't need air to burn.

The mines themselves were rudimentary – cans, jars and the like, their bases filled with powder. (Fortunately General Terry hadn't taken all the fort's gunpowder for the campaign.) Above them was broken metal, nails and, everything else failing, potsherds. They'd be effective enough but their moral effect would, Thorn hopes, be much greater. The Sioux had a great distaste for artillery and this would seem very much like it in its effects.

At last, about sunset, it was time. He had eighty mines ready, some linked in threes, some in fives, and with quickmatch fuses of various lengths to avoid them all going off at once and turning a weapon into a firework display. Hipman strolled over.

'Thank God, there's not a cloud in the sky. With luck it won't rain tomorrow either.'

'They should survive a week in the ground,

sir,' Thorn said. The mines themselves had been pitched over on top.

'Dirty way of fighting a war,' Hipman said.

'Are there any clean ones?'

Hipman laughed, then: 'I've sorted the cavalry out. Every horse in the fort will have a rider. That's sixty-three mounted men, and count on just better than half to be fully effective.' He shook his head. 'That's long odds.'

Thorn said nothing. That part had already been settled.

Then: 'Do you really think they'll come tomorrow, sir?'

Hipman considered a moment, then: 'Not being senior Union generals in the late war, they don't take to long periods of vacillation. Besides, they'll soon be out of food. They'll have to move on or acquire some. Ours. Oh, yes, they'll come tomorrow. I reckon on seven hundred of them, all in war paint and maybe a majority of them gun armed, and all of them confident of doing to us what was done to Custer.'

'But you're not Custer, sir.'

'Nor want to be. He may or may not be a "hero" but he's dead for sure. Carry on, Captain.'

'Sir!'

*

An hour after sunset the gates were opened and the first patrol went out. It was on foot and led by Sergeant Raney.

'Don't worry about making notes. If you see anything you don't like, shoot at it.'

Raney had nodded. It was his job to keep prying eyes off the mine-layers to follow but there was no need for subtlety. Only the very hardy spirits amongst the Sioux risked fighting at night and even then kept the risks to themselves down to the minimum. Gunflashes and shooting wouldn't attract them. Army soldiers marched to the sound of the guns. Indians took the other option, most of all at night.

Just leaving the mines themselves wasn't the worst part of the job. That was hiding the fuses and above all not accidentally putting a shovel through them. Thorn had kept the worst job for himself, telling everyone where to put everything, in the dark and, as it turned out, with gunflashes and screams and shouting in the background.

'No, damn it, dig deeper man. It's sticking up like a sore thumb.' And: 'What the heck, you're not burying your grandfather – an inch of earth at the most!' And then it was done and the mine-layers withdrew – the patrols would be out all night – and Thorn remained to check over the work, especially the small stones showing where the ignition points were. The men detailed to set them off tomorrow needed to find them instantly and yet nothing must risk putting off the Sioux. He decided eventually it was as good as could be managed and walked back. Hipman met him at the gate.

'You look all in,' he said. 'Get some sleep. I'll send for you when I need you.'

He nodded. It was no use expecting Hipman to get some sleep himself. He was the commander. He'd only sleep when the battle was over.

Thorn went to the quarters he was sharing with Tidyman and lay down on the bed fully clothed and booted. He was asleep within seconds of his head touching the pillow.

A soldier woke him. 'It's time, sir.'

Thorn was up instantly. 'Just what time is it, trooper?'

'Eight in the forenoon, sir.'

'The Sioux?'

'They've assembled in Canada Gap, sir. Two miles off.'

Thorn found the washstand, splashed some rather tepid water on his face, dried it off with the well-washed cotton towel provided and went outside.

The fort was strangely silent though there were people about everywhere. He saw Hipman on the parapet by the gate along with Tidyman and hurried over to join them.

'You look better,' Hipman said. 'You were asleep on your feet.'

Thorn noticed that Hipman looked well himself. The age that had so suddenly come upon him had fallen away. This was the old general back.

'They're there,' Tidyman said, pointing, and Thorn saw a mass of light cavalry approaching slowly, headed, just as they'd supposed, for the fort gate, its weakest point.

'Get to it,' Hipman said. 'Tidyman here will command the cavalry screen. I've explained it all to him. He'll take your advice but he gets to spring the trap.'

Thorn offered his hand and Tidyman took it, smiling like a kid just given a candy. Hipman had either made his career or sentenced him to death and the odds were on the latter but counting horseshoes was behind him now; he was truly a cavalryman and that was what he had joined up for.

'Go on,' Hipman said, adding uncharacteristically, 'I'm damned proud of you both.'

And Thorn found himself smiling too.

*

It was a pitifully small cavalry screen that confronted the oncoming Sioux – twenty-six men and ten men standing behind them at the forward ignition points, holding their slow-matches and waiting for the word. Thorn, deputed to give it by proxy, sat his horse by Tidyman at the northern end of the skirmish line.

'There's a lot of 'em,' Tidyman said.

There was. Getting on for 1,000, Thorn thought, though it was hard to tell. Probably most of them were armed with bows and lances but given the disparity in numbers between the forces it hardly seemed to matter.

The Sioux edged nearer, intent on imposing themselves by sheer numbers. Zanai and Little Cloud were probably surprised to find themselves confronted by horsemen outside the fort and vastly tempted by that open gate behind them.

'The Assyrian came down like the wolf on the fold, and his cohorts were gleaming in purple and gold . . .'

'That from the Bible?' Thorn asked, knowing it wasn't. If Tidyman needed verses to keep himself calm, so be it.

'Some poet I read in school. Byron, I think. But our fellows have neither gold nor purple, just feathers!'

'What happened to 'em?' Thorn persisted. 'The Assyrians, that is.'

Tidyman laughed shortly. 'They got beat.'

'So will these,' Thorn said. 'Remember, they won't go to a canter before they charge, they'll come at us hell for leather. When I give the word get your men back without delay and in a body. Stragglers will have a hard time of it.'

'And you?'

'I'll be right behind you.'

Tidyman nodded. 'You've done this before?'

'Not hardly!' Thorn said and turned once again to check on the slowmatch men. They were still in place.

'Jack!'

Thorn looked instantly to the front. The great host was stirring. They were about 150 yards off but the first ranks were spreading out. Unlike disciplined cavalry who did everything in stages – walk, canter, charge – they were charging straight off.

'Now,' he told Tidyman.

Tidyman's own order was neither complicated or formal. He just yelled:

'Back!'

But he was obeyed. Thorn didn't need to give a separate order to the ten – retreat itself was the order. Turning, he saw his men lighting the first set of fuses. He watched as they ran back to light the inner set of fuses. He only hoped the lighting of the fuses hadn't been rushed, that everything had taken.

And suddenly the noise hit him. Initially the Sioux had moved in silence but now they were calling out their war cries, each subsumed into a single great roar. He moved back, ignoring the Indians, eyes only for the fuse-men. And then their job was complete and they were sprinting back to the fort.

Except for one. He'd fallen. Thorn spurred over to him, saw he was dead; he'd taken a bullet in the forehead. Thorn hadn't even heard any shooting; it had been lost in the roar.

He dismounted and – holding the reins tightly – drew his six-gun and fired close up at the ignition point. The bullet had no effect but the fiery muzzle-cases did. He mounted again, only then glancing back.

They were maybe sixty yards behind him, moving forward like a wave of the sea, not quite full out but fast enough. He touched spurs to his horse's flanks. Something snapped past his ear – a bullet. And then another. He paid them no heed. Nobody hit anything firing from horse-back. Even the dead soldier had been hit by accident rather than by design. But there were a hell of a lot of guns behind him . . .

The gate hove into view and then he was through it, having to pull up short to avoid the mass of cavalrymen waiting just behind it, Hipman at their head. He'd made it!

'Here,' Hipman said reaching across to hand him a spare sabre. He took it, looked back at the approaching Indians, speeding up now, driven wild by the too-tempting prospect of that open gate.

There was nothing spectacular about the explosions – no great flashes of lightning, just smoke and dust and flying metal in the air . . . and falling men and horses.

Probably only a fraction of the Indian host had been affected but the charge had been halted thirty yards from the open gate and showed no signs of restarting. The Indians were hurt and confused and wanted no more, but that was not how he and Hipman had planned things.

'Charge!' Hipman shouted. 'Use your sabres!'

And Thorn charged with them. Slash! Into the still roiling mass of the halted Sioux warriors, wielding his sabre with all the prescribed viciousness of the drill book, his horse bowling over the smaller Indian ponies.

Faces flashed in front of him and he cut at them, saw blood spurt but heard nothing but the all-encompassing roar of battle. It seemed to go on for ever and few resisted strongly. The Indians had always had a fear of the 'long knives' – and rightly. Guns they had accustomed themselves to, and even mastered to an extent, but the sabres of the cavalry never ceased to terrify.

And suddenly there was no one in front of him and only bluecoats behind, at least mounted. For the Sioux had fled and he noticed now that the roar of battle had changed to a moan of collective anguish punctuated by screams.

The shooting restarted but it was the soldiers who were shooting, finishing off the wounded Indians. He should stop it – and then he recalled he wasn't an officer any more. He should ask Hipman—

'Jack!'

He turned, saw Tidyman riding towards him, his sabre loose in his hand now, dripping blood. But there was no triumph in his face.

'Jack, they've got him. He's shot and asking for you.'

'Take me to him,' Thorn said, forgetting it

wasn't his place to give orders. But Tidyman didn't question it for a second.

Hipman was dying. There was no doubt about that. He'd been shot close up – you could see the scorch marks on his blue coat – and the bullet had obviously smashed his backbone. He was bleeding badly too. But he was still conscious.

'See to the men, Tidyman,' he said weakly. And Tidyman moved off. They were past the line of the furthest mines and the ground around was fee of corpses. Once again General Hipman had led from the front. Thorn got down from his horse, knelt beside him.

'It worked, boy, it worked,' Hipman said, even his voice a shadow of its former self.

'It was the mines. Your idea, sir.'

'You execution, Jack, and you thought of the sabre attack too. And put it all together. However much they feared the long knives they still had the numbers to overwhelm us, but the combination . . .' He broke off, coughed up blood.

'Don't try to—'

'No, let me speak. It won't harm much now.' He paused, then: 'It was a kid that got me – fifteen or sixteen. I doubt he'd ever fired a gun before. I didn't kill him ... But it's not that. There's something I have to tell you.'

'Sir?'

'I asked her to marry me, Jack. Before the telegram when I thought I still had a life.' He coughed again and his voice was weaker when he continued. 'Why not? I asked myself. She had no one, just as I had no one. But whatever else, I could offer her my protection.'

'Sir, I—'

'Listen, Jack. I had no chance. She's besotted with the young hero who rode with her through the night. Only fair, Jack, only right. I still thought there was a chance so I fixed the job at the fort for her. If I couldn't have her, I could at least help her. But I can't help her now, Jack. See she comes to no harm ...'

And suddenly it was over, a gout of blood, the cessation of breath.

Thorn stood up, noticing that he was still holding the sabre he had wielded to such effect only minutes before. Then he saw Tidyman twenty feet back. Behind him the killing was about over save for the dispatching of wounded horses.

He'd done nothing about the human slaughter. He shrugged mentally. No cavalryman had survived on the Little Big Horn. Only Hipman could have given an order to take prisoners and make it stick and they'd killed him.

He walked over to join Tidyman, leading his horse.

'The General's dead,' he said. 'You're in command now.'

Tidyman looked suddenly lost. A touch of grief, Thorn guessed, but more the weight of responsibility now resting on his shoulders.

'What the hell do I do?' he said.

'It's mostly done,' Thorn said reasonably. He added: 'Send a dispatch rider to General Terry and let him know about all this. But mention I was here only later, and only if asked – even then, I was just here for the ride. General Terry wouldn't thank you for more, believe me. I'm a civilian after all.' He shook his head. 'I don't need credit or glory or whatever.'

Tidyman nodded.

'It was his last victory,' Thorn added. 'Make it so in your dispatch. And bury him here where he fell – William Hipman, Brigadier-General, USA.'

'I promise you that.'

'I've another promise I want from you,' Thorn said, unbuttoning his coat and then his shirt to extract a money-belt which he handed to Tidyman.

'Give that to Miss Roman. Tell her it was

General Hipman's last wish that she have it. Don't take no for an answer.'

'She'll surely refuse—'

'Don't let her. It was the General's *last* wish.' He paused. 'That's true in its way, believe me.'

'You mean . . . the proposal.'

Thorn nodded. 'He tell you?'

'It's a small fort.' He paused. 'She'll not want to take it but I reckon if I lay the moral blackmail on thick enough she'll have to take it. I'll do it. You've earned that favour and more.'

'Thanks,' Thorn said. 'I reckon you'll be OK now. The Sioux won't regroup this side of hell. The fort's safe.'

'It was my first battle,' Tidyman admitted suddenly.

'I didn't guess,' Thorn lied, and stuck out his hand. 'I'll ride with you any time, Bill.'

'An honour, Jack.'

And then Thorn mounted up again and rode his tired horse away from the field of honour, which much more resembled a charnel house. He looked back only once to where Hipman lay. He didn't salute. Hipman was dead, indifferent to that or any other gesture, but he'd died a general again and at the head of his troops.

As for Jane . . . well, Bill Tidyman would keep

his word and so he'd kept his unspoken word to Hipman. As for himself . . .

He shook his head. There was no time for regrets. He had a job to do, a man still to find and kill.

SEVEN

Thorn guessed that Chiles's first thought would be to go straight for Canada and lose himself, but he no longer had the financial resources to do it. Thorn guessed denying him the money had hurt him worse than the bullet because it meant he had to steal more, and he surely wasn't about to do that in Canada. If he intended to settle down there, or even hide away for any length of time, the last thing he needed was to be on a wanted list there. So he needed to get some money together now, here in the States, and quickly.

On the night after the battle Thorn slept like the dead of the same and only awoke about noon to find his horse patiently cropping the grass. He made a noon meal of pemmican and coffee and then set himself to thinking things through over a cigar. After a while he dug out his map.

There wasn't much due north between here and the Canadian border, and for once the greater population was in Canada, with Lake Winnipeg and the hamlets of Potage La Prairie. A good place to start from for a fugitive – west to Saskatchewan, north-east to Manitoba and east to Ontario. A clever man could lose himself easily in all that space, given funds. But the loss of the satchel had made it urgent for Chiles to turn thief again. Where?

There were a few names on the map in the north this side of the border but Thorn suspected they were just names, not places of any account, which was to say, wealth. So Chiles had to go east. And as he would be certain he was being followed he'd avoid the obvious places in the first instance, preferring the out of the way places that still had promise of some stealable wealth. And he'd need a doctor too, for that shoulder wound.

Thorn let his finger rove over the map. It wasn't like the conventional method of cutting trail and following tracks but truth to tell that was always a problematical procedure. Usually, success depended on getting into the mind of your prey, thinking his thoughts.

Getting into Chiles's mind ought to be hard but wasn't. He didn't need to think of that first crime itself, just remember that Chiles was a hunted criminal and, no less important, that he was clever. And arrogant.

Yet there'd be no double bluffs because he would naturally presume his hunter was clever enough to discount the too obvious. So it would be somewhere out of the way, small but not too small . . .

His finger lighted on a place – Challiter City . . . Thorn formed the words in his mind but he did not speak them. Still, the phantom sentence seemed reasonable. But then, so would . . . Chiles went to Gritches Hole. Or Chiles went to Wilson's Ford or Tophet Township. . . .

All the same, he liked that unspoken first sentence best. Call it instinctive, a gut feeling, or just a belief in his own luck but he more than half-believed it. And lucky he was, in a left-handed sort of way. He'd started out with thirteen names and now there was just the one left – Chiles's own.

All that said, he could be making a mistake, and if he were, it would mean Chiles would slip through his fingers again, and this time it would probably be for ever. Lucky or not, you only got so many chances and he'd had Charlie Chiles in his sights once already. He had to be right.

He noticed that his cigar had gone out. He relit it. It was his last and the chances were that such cigars as he'd be able to get in Challiter City would not be up to much.

Challiter City was the classic one-horse town. Why not a one-saloon town, Thorn thought idly as he rode in, but of course no such thing could ever exist. A place with a single saloon wasn't a town – it was a roadhouse. Even Challiter, which had neither bank, deputy sheriff's office or city hall, still had three saloons. And a town marshal's office, albeit a lean-to on the side of the Fat Chance saloon, the biggest of the three and with a fancy sign that read: 'Fine Liquors Sold Here'. He made a beeline for the office.

Fred Digby was sixty years old, wore an ancient cap and ball six-shooter on his belt and was very fat indeed though with a hint of muscle under the blubber. He offered Thorn a mug of coffee and a seat as soon as he entered the tiny office and he examined the proffered dodger with interest. Thorn guessed he was pretty honest as town marshals went. A dishonest one should have made enough to be living high on the hog in San Francisco by his age. And so it proved.

'I reckon I've met this feller recently,' Digby

said, 'but this dodger is pretty old.'

'It's still valid.'

Digby smiled. 'Depends how you look at things,' he said. 'It's really just a statement of wants, not an indictment or a conviction. You wouldn't be some bounty hunter now, would you?' Thorn understood. Digby didn't like the idea of destroying a man for an ancient offence, a man who might well have changed over the years. And doing it only for money. The only thing for it was to be open with him.

Digby listened carefully, not interrupting once. Then: 'I don't blame you, young fella, but you've spent too much time on him. There's a time to move on . . . but not now. I don't like men who sell guns to Indians, no sir.'

'When was he here?'

'He came two days back. He waltzed into the saloon asking for a doctor. I had words with him – always do with men with gunshot wounds. He said he'd run into a couple of Sioux out on the prairie and driven them off. I believed him.

'And?'

'As I said, I believed him. I sent for Doc Clare, he saw to him, the fella spent the night in town and only rode out again yesterday morning, bright and early too.

'You wouldn't happen to know where?'

Digby shrugged. 'I saw him in the bar next door and just the once, a few minutes at most. I couldn't even telegraph the county seat to warn about the Indians. The lines have been down these past five days. Come to think of it, it's just as well I didn't telegraph as it turned out to be a lie.' He paused. 'You don't reckon any of those Sioux will be coming this way?'

Thorn shook his head. 'They'll be heading for Canada direct, going due north. So will Sitting Bull and Crazy Horse and the rest. Custer sent the Gatling guns back to Fort Abe Lincoln but you can reckon for certain sure General Terry won't repeat that mistake and that the Sioux know it, and know what those things can do.'

'Poor devils!' Digby said, unexpectedly.

'You feel sorry for them?'

'They're overmatched, caught between the rock and the hard place.' Digby paused. 'But I'll feel safer when they're in Canada or dead. Guess that makes me a hypocrite.'

Thorn shook his head. 'I'd call it Christian charity tempered by common sense.'

Digby laughed.

'Tell me about Doc Clare,' Thorn said.

The surgery – in reality Clare's own house – was at the end of a narrow alley leading off at right angles to Main Street. A hand-painted sign proclaimed its function and there was a bell by the door.

'It doesn't work,' Digby said. 'The noise got on his nerves. He took the clapper out. You have to knock.'

Thorn knocked and after some delay a small, rather shambling figure confronted them. His dress suited his profession, dark coat and trousers, a white shirt and thin cravat, currently loose. There was a strong smell of alcohol too but Clare didn't seem drunk. Digby spoke first:

'It's about your patient of two days back. Official business.'

'Mr Smith, you mean?' Clare smiled rather gnomically, shuffled back. 'You'd better come in.'

The room they were taken to was clean but every available surface was cluttered, with books, medical equipment, bottles and jars of materia medica and the like. Thorn guessed there was no current Mrs Clare.

'Sit, if you like,' Clare said, not sitting down himself.

'We'll stand,' Digby said, obviously not trusting himself to the rickety chairs. 'It turned out your Mr Smith lied. He was shot by the army, not Indians. He was running guns to the Sioux.'

Clare looked to Thorn. 'By a Winchester?'

Thorn nodded.

'Interesting,' Clare said. 'I thought so. He said it was by a stolen pistol but it had gone straight through so I thought not. Nice to have it confirmed.'

'How badly was he hurt?'

'I'm not sure I can answer that, Mr . . .'

'Thorn, Jack Thorn.'

'It's official, as I said,' Digby added.

Clare shrugged. 'In that case I'll tell you. Not badly. The bullet grazed a rib and some shreds of clothing lodged in the shoulder muscle but it missed the clavicle. Nothing broken. He'd thought the bullet was still in and had tried to prise it out himself and, naturally, had failed.'

'So what did you do?'

'I extracted several nasty bits of clothing, cleaned it and sealed the wound for him.'

'But he was fit enough to ride on.'

Clare shook his head. 'He thought he was, and did in fact do so, but he wasn't. He'd a low fever from the dirt carried into the wound initially. I told him to rest for a week. He didn't.' Clare paused. 'Incidentally, he didn't pay his bill either.' He looked rather hopefully at Thorn.

'Have you any idea where he went?' Thorn

asked. It was up to Clare himself to collect on his own work.

'He did not vouchsafe that information to me, gentlemen.'

'How would riding affect him?' Digby asked astutely.

'It would have made the fever worse. The truth is, it's impossible to say for certain but my guess is that he will be feverish for a week. But I reckon he could function – below par, but function. A very tough *hombre* indeed, Mr Smith.'

'Didn't you talk at all?' Thorn asked.

'Of course. He stayed overnight in my house. I converse politely with my guests.'

'And he gave no indication of where he was headed?'

'Around the territory, he said. He was searching for land for a horse ranch. He was particularly interested in the local towns, which had a reliable bank and the like.'

'And?'

'I told him the truth. Only Nike City has a bank of the sort a sensible man would risk putting his money into. I have an account there myself . . .' He broke off. 'You think he meant to stage a robbery?'

'It's possible,' Thorn said.

'Foolish of me,' Clare said, shaking his head as

he chided himself. 'But in the end, of no real account.'

'Why?'

'He might feel he was fit to do anything but he wasn't. People with low fevers rarely are. And after riding so far, the fever might well be not all that low. I told him to rest and he wilfully disobeyed me. Decamped without paying his bill.' He shook his head. 'That's the trouble with treating transients. Why pay when you can ride?'

Outside, Thorn commented on the fact that Clare hadn't seemed in the least drunk, which Digby had suggested he would be.

'Wrong,' Digby said. 'He was drunk all right.' He paused. 'He's a good doctor even when drunk. Which is just as well as he always is drunk, has been since he was a Union surgeon in the war to hear him tell it. And what other kind of doctor would you get in a town this size out in the back of beyond?'

Thorn said: 'I'll be obliged if you'll point me towards the county seat – Nike City.'

'I'll do better, lad. I'll accompany you. It's not advertised but I'm also a deputy sheriff at twenty dollars a month. I'd prefer to keep it, and if I don't show up and warn Bull Gunder, I won't.'

Thorn smiled slightly.

'This is a poor town, lad. The mine's almost run down and since the war the demand for horses is easier supplied from Kentucky and Virginia. We sell at lower prices than before but our supplies from back East are high still because of the trouble it takes to transport them. We just scrape along.'

'I didn't doubt you for a moment,' Thorn said, amused despite himself and elated too. Chiles, who had almost been out of his grasp, was virtually in it again. 'But when we meet up with Chiles, leave him to me.'

Digby laughed. 'You think I'd be too slow drawing my old percussion pistol? Well, you're probably right. But I don't go in for drawing at all. When I go into action it's with a sawn-off Greener in my hand, and I'm pretty damn useful still, believe me.'

The picture of an angry Fred Digby with a short, double-barrelled shotgun the words had conjured up in Thorn's mind dispelled any illusion that he wasn't.

'I'll get a rig. I'm too old for saddles,' Digby said. 'Besides, your horse could do with a few hours without you on its back. That'll be five dollars.'

Thorn paid him. 'You don't have a share in the livery too?' he asked.

'No,' Digby said, 'that I own outright.'

It was a four-hour drive to Nike City. Thorn was happy to let Digby take the reins. He drove at a medium pace, giving Thorn's horse, tied up behind, an easy journey. Thorn found the hard, unsprung seat distinctly uncomfortable. He disliked trains too, especially when he was obliged to hold conversations with inquisitive strangers. But here Digby did most of the talking, mostly about his town, and yet little by little he seemed to worm everything out about Thorn's life.

'A word of advice, lad,' Digby said, 'from an old hunter. After a long chase when you finally find your prey and he's sick with fever and tired of running, what follows might seem inevitable. His luck's run out and yours is overflowing. But that's when you have to be most careful of all. Luck's just oddness, plain cussedness, and the inevitable is only that afterwards.'

'Very philosophical,' Thorn said, not altogether appreciatively.

'A hobby. I like a good, deep book – all the more so since I found myself suddenly old. It comes on you like that. One day the bottle still has plenty in it, the next and you realize more of it's gone than you realize. You ain't there yet, boy, but maybe it'll feel like that when this Charlie Chiles is gone from your life.'

That was very possibly true, but Thorn said nothing.

'But as I said, assume nothing. It ain't happened yet.'

Which, Thorn thought, like all the philosophy he'd read, was obvious anyway when true and of damned little use otherwise. 'Tell me about Bull Gunder.'

'His names told you everything. And that's only what his friends call him. "Pig" is what his detractors prefer. Not too unfairly either, but "boar" would be more exact. Ever hunt wild boar?'

'No.'

'They look a little like common or garden hogs, a touch hairier, but they're implacable killers in a snuffling sort of way. If you ain't hunting 'em, avoid them.' He raised a hand briefly. 'That's it, Nike City.'

Thorn hadn't paid much attention to the view. It didn't change, just poverty grass to the horizon and a few distant stands of weary-looking trees. But now he saw it – several miles off, a slew of buildings clustering together as if they were lonely under the big sky.

'Walk soft in Nike City,' Digby said suddenly. 'I

do.' And he was silent for the remainder of the drive.

It was bigger than he'd guessed, than it looked. Probably being county seat made the difference, sucking business away from the other towns, leaving people there to count their pennies.

The trail didn't run straight into Main Street but circled around a hummock that seemed to rise up out of the land as they approached, so they saw only the backs of buildings, houses, saloons, brothels, what have you, and not a face at any window.

But the town wasn't silent. It sounded like there was a fair being held somewhere. And then they came in line with Main Street and he saw the crowd about the livery stable and the pole crane used for lifting hay now holding up a different cargo – a man, arms tied to his sides but his legs free. His hair was red and there was also a scar on his face. They were lynching Charlie Chiles!

'No!' Thorn said, reaching for his six-gun but he never drew it. Digby leaned across, caught his gun hand in his own. It was like being in a steel vice.

'Let be,' he said softly. 'There's nothing you can do. Or should. It's no lynching. They always use the livery for official hangings. There'll have been a trial.'

Thorn didn't know whether he was lying but it scarcely mattered now. Chiles had stopped kicking. Whether they'd come on it at the end and he'd plain suffocated or whether the rope had broken his neck he didn't know. And it could have been official. At least, nobody bothered to put a shot into the swinging body.

'You OK now?' Digby asked.

'Yeah.'

Digby released him, instantly turning the rig down one of the alleys leading off Main Street, driving to the near-abandoned end of it, strewn with rubbish, beyond which could be seen the seemingly never-ending grass cover of the prairie.

'Stay here. Anybody comes, you're waiting for me. But they won't. Can I trust you?'

Thorn nodded.

After a while Thorn took out one of the black cigars he'd bought in the bar in Challiter City, lit it. It tasted foul but he persevered.

Why? he asked himself. He'd wanted him dead. Was it because he'd wanted to do it himself? But he knew it wasn't that, though kill him he would have. It was . . .

148

He'd no words for it. He changed hands with the cigar. Where Digby had gripped him, he hurt. The man had the strength of a bear.

After about half an hour, Digby returned, climbed aboard and set the rig in motion, back the way they'd come.

'He tried to rob the bank,' Digby said. 'Shot the teller but bungled the getaway. They don't know who he is, reckon he's just some saddle bum down on his luck. I didn't enlighten them.'

'Thanks for what you did back there,' Thorn said. 'I reckon you saved me some embarrassment.'

'Like hell; if you'd interfered they'd have hung you too.'

And Thorn found himself believing him.

'So it was a lynching.'

'Depends on how you call it. He did have a trial in front of the mayor. Technically he's a magistrate and not empowered to try felonies, but . . .' He shrugged, adding: 'Nobody'll give a damn.'

Not even me, Thorn thought. The spasm was over. He felt a little on the hollow side but no longer angry. In a way it was an all too appropriate end for Charlie Chiles.

'By the way,' Digby said, 'they were dividing up his property when I got to the office. Bull

Gunder got the money, the chief deputy got the horse, another deputy his gun. There was nothing else left but this.' He dug into his pocket and pulled out a notebook which Thorn took. 'Maybe it'll be of interest.'

'I'm obliged,' Thorn said.

'I think you are,' Digby said. 'The dodger mentioned three thousand dollars' reward.'

'That should go to Bull Gunder,' Thorn said, smiling slightly.

'If you reckon so.'

'Damn him!' Thorn said viciously. Then, more softly: 'You can have it. But there's no bank in Challiter City. Turn about and take me to the one in Nike City and I'll get you cash.'

'Like hell. Gunder would find out. Instruct your bank to put it into my account in Chicago. I've written the details on the last page of the notebook. It was blank.'

'You trust me that much?'

'Yes. For you it's a debt of honour. Besides, I reckon you can well afford it. You're a rich man.'

'Why do you say that?'

'I saw the letter of credit in your wallet when you took out the dodger back in my office. I couldn't see the limit but poor folks just don't have letters of credit.'

'I'll do it,' Thorn said. 'Stop the rig.'

'Why?'

'I'm going home,' Thorn said.

'About time,' Digby said. He brought the rig to a halt and offered his hand. 'You've agreed to pay me so you don't have to take it.'

Thorn grasped his hand. 'Thanks, *compadre*,' he said.

'*De nada*,' Digby replied.

EPILOGUE

Thorn took his time. There was no longer any urgency in his life. On the second day of his return journey he finally brought himself to look at Chiles's book – and found it wasn't his but Roman's.

He unbridled his horse, hitched it long to a stunted bush with his lariat so it could cross the grass with some liberty, and settled down to reading.

Except it made no real sense to him – what were deictic pronouns, optative systems, second perfectives and the like? Overall it seemed to be an attempt to prove that Azat was a language akin to Greek and Latin but much older. Either Roman was brilliant or he was a crank and Thorn had no way to tell the difference. More likely it was the latter but he couldn't be certain and even if it were just a one in a hundred chance, should he let Roman acquire even posthumous fame and honour? No. His treason could be forgotten because it had been foiled but it could never be rewarded. He tore the back page out of the notebook and burnt the rest. Maybe science was the poorer for it but he felt no guilt at all.

And not just that. He realized part of what had been driving him was guilt at not having been with his wife and child when they needed him so desperately. That too was gone. Now they were at peace and so was he.

He had to pass the fort to get to the nearest railhead. He would have preferred to avoid it but there was something he needed to check – had Tidyman done right by Hipman? The dead don't care but he found he did.

Tidyman had been as good as his word. Where he had fallen there was now a wooden head-board on which, carefully if inexpertly painted in white, was the inscription:

WILLIAM HIPMAN
Brigadier-General
USA
pro patria

It was enough. He would have gone on then if

he hadn't seen a rider from the fort coming towards him at the gallop. It turned out to be Tidyman.

'Congratulations, Captain,' Thorn said, glancing at the fresh new bars.

'Field promotion, given by General Terry.'

'He's been to the fort?'

'Came yesterday. He's still here now and he's the one who sent me. He wants words with you.'

Thorn shrugged. 'Why not?' Only a fool refused an invitation from a general in federal territory.

'About the money belt . . .' Thorn began.

'She took it, Jack,' Tidyman said, almost smiling.

Thorn didn't press him. It was probably for the best.

'What about Chiles?' Tidyman asked.

'He'll do no more gun-running.'

Tidyman nodded, then: 'Let's not keep the general waiting.'

'Heck, I'm a civilian. I can afford to do that much.'

But he didn't.

The fort was bustling. Terry had brought two full troops with him but he kept him waiting in the outer office only long enough to exchange a few private words with the new-minted captain who then emerged to direct him inwards.

'It seems the army owes you a double debt of gratitude, Thorn,' General Terry said shaking his hand.

'It owes General Hipman a rather more profound one.'

'Ah, yes. Sit down, please.'

Which it wasn't about to pay, Thorn thought.

'It's a problem,' Terry said. 'We can't afford another dead general. I know Custer was a light colonel but the newspapers prefer the old wartime rank. So Major Hipman died with honour but in a skirmish. Though the grave stays as it is. Captain Tidyman promised that and I'll abide by his word.'

And now he wants to know if I'm going to kick up a fuss. He said:

'William Hipman always put the army first when he was alive. In death . . . likewise.'

And the interview was effectively over. Terry even offered him a commission but didn't seem displeased when it was refused, and maybe he was even a little relieved when Thorn took his leave. So much for the gratitude of great institutions.

Tidyman was waiting for him outside and instantly latched on to him. Hadn't he a fort to command? But Thorn didn't ask the question. Theoretically, yes, but with Terry here being fort commander was to be more decorative than essential, like a fob on a watch-chain.

Thorn found himself outside the storeroom that had served as a schoolroom.

'It's a hospital now. She helped out with the wounded until Terry arrived, then she wasn't needed. She left the fort.'

'So be it,' Thorn said. He'd left without a word after the battle. Jane had returned the compliment. But Tidyman was smiling.

'She did say she'd be staying with the Kefauvers in Lucky Nugget.'

Kefauver and son had been very interested in the battle and Chiles's death but after the bare minimum of questioning Mrs Kefauver ushered them both out of the room, then left it herself. The pair were to be left alone.

'Hipman told me about his proposal,' Thorn said after a moment, not knowing where to begin.

'He was very charming,' Jane said. 'Poor man.'

'He said . . .' Thorn broke off, then: 'The belt was from me, Jane. I'm sorry about the lie.'

'It wasn't much of one. Tidyman insisted it was Hipman's bequest to me – you made him do that, didn't you? – but it was impossible to believe. Hipman wasn't fat but he could never have put that belt around him.'

Thorn hadn't thought of that. He said: 'It was the first thing that came into my mind. He died asking me to look after you.'

And suddenly Jane was in tears. He went to her.

'He was kind to me,' Jane said. 'I'm sorry . . .'

'Don't be,' Thorn said. 'Nobody else has shed tears for him. It was . . .'

And suddenly she was in his arms and Hipman and the Sioux and Charlie Chiles were quite forgotten.